SANTA FE SUNRISE

SANTA FE SUNRISE

•

Kathleen Fuller

AVALON BOOKS
NEW YORK

PRINTED IN THE UNITED STATES OF AMERICA
ON ACID-FREE PAPER
BY HADDON CRAFTSMEN, BLOOMSBURG, PENNSYLVANIA

To my three precious gifts from God:
Mathew, Sydney, and Zoie. I love you.

Chapter One

Santa Fe, New Mexico Territory
May, 1849 –

Luke Jackson steadily eyed his commanding officer. Moments ago he had been summoned to the
small adobe house that served as the Army's head-
quarters. Apprehension filled him at the sight of
Captain LaFevre's serious expression, but he
tamped the emotion down, keeping his own features
blank. He'd had his heart set on leaving New
Mexico—and the American Army—within the
hour, and had planned to return home to Texas. After a year and a half of military service, he was
more than ready. The Treaty of Guadalupe Hildago

had been signed a few months ago, and now freedom was within his grasp.

At least he thought it was.

Captain LaFevre placed his hands behind his back, his posture rigid. Everything about the officer was precise, from the thin, meticulously trimmed black mustache that lined his upper lip to the pristine white sashes cutting two smooth diagonal lines across his dark blue uniform. LaFevre was a man who commanded respect, and Luke had never had a problem giving it to him. He counted himself privileged to have served under such an officer for the past twelve months.

But the war against Mexico had taken its toll on everyone, especially Luke. He fought the urge to rub his hand across his right thigh, something he did whenever it ached. Although the bullet wound had healed three weeks ago, the pain often returned, making his limp more pronounced. Fortunately, all he had to do at the moment was stand at attention while LaFevre explained his orders.

"You have served your country well, *Monsieur* Jackson," LaFevre said, his French accent lacing his words. "I know you are looking forward to returning to San Jose."

"San Antonio," Luke corrected in a low, firm voice. "Texas, sir."

"*Pardon,*" LaFevre replied. "Sometimes I get these Spanish names confused."

"No problem, sir."

LaFevre stepped out from behind his desk and passed through the bright beam of sunlight streaming through the window. The light enveloped the clay house in a soft, sienna-colored glow. He stopped directly in front of Luke, who had to look down at the much shorter man. "I realize that as a volunteer, your term of service has ended. Because of this, I am reluctant to give you new orders, but I have no choice. You are the only man under my command suited for this particular job."

Luke's curiosity was piqued. "Job, sir?"

"Colonel Washington has asked a favor," LaFevre said, referring to the highest ranking official in the New Mexico Territory. "It seems that his friend, Herman Faraday, has requested a military escort for his daughter and her companion. She will be traveling from here to Las Vegas. I have chosen you to be her escort. After you see *Mademoiselle* Faraday safely to her destination, you will receive your discharge."

"I can return to Texas?"

"*Oui.*"

A tiny wave of relief flowed through Luke. Las Vegas, in the western part of the New Mexico Territory, was about 60 miles from Santa Fe. A five-day journey at the most. But one thing puzzled him. "Why me, sir? If I may ask?"

The captain paused. "I have come to believe you are a man of honor, *Monsieur* Jackson. You fought valiantly in battle, and you are dependable. There are not many men in my division I would entrust to travel with a young woman, even if she is properly chaperoned." He smoothed one side of his pencil thin moustache with his index finger as he regarded Luke. "I know Miss Faraday will be safe under your guard."

"I thank you for the vote of confidence, sir," Luke said, standing a little straighter. "When will we be leaving?"

LaFevre turned and picked up a piece of paper off his desk. "Here are the specifics," he said, handing it to Luke.

Scanning the page, Luke saw the date, time and place he was to meet the Faradays. Tomorrow morning at the Hotel LaFonda. "Is there anything else I should know, sir?"

LaFevre looked at him solemnly. "There has been an increase in Indian attacks along the trail in the past weeks. Several travelers have been wounded or killed in the raids. *Monsieur* Faraday was wise to want an escort for his daughter."

A wave of dread flowed over Luke, but he forced the emotion away. He'd survived many battles, including Contreras and Cherubusco. And in the months since the war had ended, the desire to return home had increased with each passing day. He wouldn't let a band of rogue Indians keep him from returning to San Antonio. Not after all he'd been through the past eighteen months.

The captain placed his hand on Luke's arm, his stern countenance softening. *"Adieu,* Luke," he said quietly. "And *bonne chance."*

Under LaFevre's command Luke had learned quite a bit of French, although he was more comfortable speaking English or Spanish. *"Merci, mon Capitan,"* he replied, knowing full well he would need more than luck if he and Miss Faraday were to make it safely to Las Vegas.

"Senorita, I fear you are making a bad mistake."

Melanie Faraday turned to Flora Fuentes, the housekeeper her father had hired two months ago when they first arrived in Santa Fe. The older woman's creased features were shadowed with apprehension. Melanie laid a hand on her arm to reassure her.

"Everything will be fine, Flora," she said, taking her green cloak from the woman's hand. "I have faith that it will."

"I wish I felt the same," Flora mumbled, stepping away from Melanie and grabbing a broom. She began sweeping the floor of the villa with furious strokes. "You're *papa* will not be pleased. And what about *Senor* Vincent?"

"I'll worry about them later," Melanie said, hurrying to the door. "Remember our plan."

"How can I forget?" A puff of dust swirled around Flora's ankles.

Breathing a sigh of relief, Melanie opened the door. "*Gracias,* Flora. I'll see you soon," she said, escaping the villa before the housekeeper had a chance to reply.

Twenty minutes later, Melanie walked through the lobby of the Hotel LaFonda. Looking around, she snapped open her fan and briskly waved it in front of her face, ignoring the early morning chill that consumed her. She paced the length of the room, anxiety pooling in her stomach, yet tempered by the slightest tinge of excitement. Who would have thought that she—the predictable, obedient daughter of a wealthy Boston businessman—could be capable of doing something so out of character? So impulsive? So—

So stupid, she thought nervously, casting a glance at the entry of the hotel. The muscles in her wrist began to burn as she flicked her fan back and forth, but she had to do something with her hands. She needed to keep herself occupied, lest she come to her senses and bolt out the door, never to look back.

The image of four young, somber faces flashed through her mind, and she knew she couldn't leave. What she was doing was right, even if her methods were a tad . . . unorthodox. Surely her father would understand, once she explained the circumstances to him. But at the moment her father was the least of her concerns, for her escort was due to arrive shortly. And she hadn't the slightest idea what she was going to say to him.

Melanie sneezed. She halted, and with her free hand she pulled out a handkerchief from the cuff of her opposite sleeve, bringing the fine linen cloth to her nose. She'd been in Santa Fe since March and she was still affected by the sandy-red dust that seemed to be everywhere.

The New Mexico Territory was completely different from her home in an exclusive neighborhood of Boston. She'd been stunned when her father had announced they were moving out West. Now that the Mexican War was over, Herman Faraday was taking advantage of his friendship with the acting governor of the territory, Colonel John Washington, who was headquartered in Santa Fe.

During the long journey on the Santa Fe Trail, her father had talked nonstop of the endless business opportunities to be had in New Mexico and other parts of the West. Although the subject of business normally bored her beyond belief, she couldn't help but be caught up in his enthusiasm. For the first time in her life she was venturing beyond the smothering confines of Boston society. She found the idea thrilling.

Until she'd discovered the true reason Herman Faraday had wanted them to move to Santa Fe, and her excitement instantly evaporated.

Ethan Vincent's image entered her mind. Dread soured her stomach at the thought of the man she had met a mere week ago. That same day she learned that, thanks to her father, Mr. Vincent was now her fiancé. Although he was pleasant looking and appeared to have a kind disposition, Melanie found it appalling that she was betrothed to a complete stranger, even if he was the son of her father's new business partner. She'd also been flabbergasted that her father would do such a thing without consulting her first. It was so unlike him.

But she didn't want to focus on that now. At the moment she needed to concentrate on the task at hand.

The distinct knock of boot heels against the wood plank floor caused her to look at the doorway again. A tall, lanky man entered the lobby wearing a long oilskin duster. His weather-beaten military hat pulled low over his brow, he lifted his chin as he scanned the nearly empty room.

He glanced in the direction of a man slumped on a ripped, faded settee in the back corner of the room. A frown formed on his shadowy face as he gave him a cursory glance before turning to Melanie. When his gaze rested on her, he whipped off his hat, revealing a tousled mane of sun-streaked brown hair.

Melanie began to fan herself in earnest.

She wasn't sure who she had expected the Army

would send, but it certainly wasn't the handsome soldier standing ten feet in front of her. As he approached, she could see he had the stoic demeanor of a man sure of himself and of his mission.

She could also see he had a limp.

It wasn't overly conspicuous, but it was detectable. Undoubtedly he had injured his leg in the war. Her heart suddenly squeezed at the thought of this man being wounded. She gave her head a quick shake, bewildered that a total stranger could affect her so deeply.

"Miss Faraday?" he asked in a low, resonant drawl.

She cleared her throat and folded her fan, determined to keep her wits about her. "Yes, I'm Miss Faraday."

"Luke Jackson, ma'am. I'm here to escort you to Las Vegas." He glanced around the room. "Where is Mr. Faraday?"

Melanie twisted the fan with her hands. "Well, uh, you see Mr. Jackson," she stammered, hesitant to reveal the truth. She tried to come up with a plausible excuse for why her father wasn't there to see her off. "He's . . . not here."

His frown deepened. "I can see that. When will he be back?"

Next week, she thought, but she knew she couldn't tell him that without him asking too many questions. Her father had traveled to Albuquerque with

Ethan the day before to meet some potential business contacts, leaving her in the care of Flora.

Melanie began to feel her resolve fading again, wilting beneath the intense scrutiny of Mr. Jackson's mahogany eyes. She prayed silently for the courage to continue. "My father was unexpectedly called out of town," she replied, wincing inwardly at the half-truth she was telling this man.

"And he allowed you to wait here alone? Without a chaperone?"

Melanie bristled at the soldier's condescending tone, never mind that her father would have reacted the exact same way if he had known what she was up to. She tilted her chin slightly. "I'm perfectly capable of waiting by myself for a few minutes. Especially in the public lobby of a hotel."

She saw Mr. Jackson glance at the unconscious man in the back of the room. An empty liquor bottle lay beside him on the settee, and two flies were circling around his head. The smell of tobacco smoke and the sound of his intoxicated snores permeated the air. For the first time Melanie noticed the saloon adjacent to the lobby. She'd been so steeped in her own thoughts that she hadn't paid close attention to her surroundings.

"I'd reckon your father would have more sense than to let a lady wait alone in a place like this," Mr. Jackson said, returning his attention to her.

"My father's sense is impeccable," she parried,

feeling a need to defend him, despite being annoyed with him over the situation with Ethan. "For your information, he did arrange a chaperone for me, but unfortunately she's been . . . detained. She'll be along shortly."

A stab of guilt ran through Melanie. She hated involving Flora in her plan, but it couldn't be helped. It would be impossible for Melanie to pull this off alone.

Mr. Jackson looked at her doubtfully, as if he didn't believe a word she'd said. His eyes were like shards of opaque brown glass, but the tiny lines near the outside corners of them indicated a man who at one time must have smiled and laughed a lot. His lips were pressed in a grim line. He was neither smiling nor laughing now.

An involuntary shiver ran down Melanie's spine. She gripped her fan so tightly in her hands the wooden handle snapped in two.

Flora's words reverberated in Melanie's head. She had a dreadful feeling the woman was right— she was making a terrible mistake.

Chapter Two

Luke glanced down at the broken fan clutched in Melanie's hands, a suspicious look creeping into his eyes. "Where did you say your father was again?" He glanced pointedly at the ruined pieces of smooth wood and ornate silk she was holding.

Melanie quickly thrust her hands behind her back. "He's on a business trip."

"Where?" he asked again, more insistently this time.

"Albuquerque." She took a step backward.

He moved a few inches forward, his large, lean frame towering over her. "Why are you going to Las Vegas?" he demanded.

"T-to visit a friend," she stammered, moving back again. His interrogation, along with his closeness, unnerved her, making her feel trapped. Disliking the sensation, she steeled herself again. "Please, I must insist that we leave Santa Fe as soon as possible."

"You seem to be in an awful hurry."

She took another step away, her back making contact with the rough textured wall of the hotel. The coldness of the adobe wall seeped through her wool cloak. "I have an ample supply of money, Mr. Jackson," she said, ignoring his comment. "More than enough to pay for a wagon and supplies."

"Hasn't your father taken care of that already?"

"Um, not exactly," she said, her voice barely above a whisper.

He shoved his hand through his hair, disheveling the burnished layers even more. "Why not?"

Yes, why not? Melanie thought distractedly, searching her mind for yet another explanation, realizing she hadn't thought her plan through at all. Whatever possessed her to attempt this in the first place?

"Something's not right here, Miss Faraday. If your father went through the trouble of arranging a military escort, why wouldn't he have made all the preparations for the trip?" Luke's frown deepened. "Do you mind explaining to me what's really going on?"

Her spirits sank, and she stared down at the chipped tile floor. So much for doing something on the spur of the moment. She should have known better than to try to circumvent her father.

"*Senorita* Faraday!" Flora shouted as she hurried into the hotel.

Melanie's eyes widened at the alarm in Flora's voice. She stepped around Luke and saw the short plump woman rushing toward her. Melanie spied the bundle in her chaperone's arms as piercing wails reached her ears.

"*Dios mio! Senorita,* the baby, she will not stop crying. I try feeding her, changing her . . . *nada.*" Flora shook her head in defeat. "She wants her *mama.*"

Without thinking, Melanie shoved her broken fan at Luke and took the infant from Flora. She cuddled the baby against her chest. "It's all right, sweetheart," she cooed, planting a kiss on the child's smooth forehead. She rocked her back and forth, whispering words of comfort close to the baby's ear, until her cries finally began to subside. "Everything will be just fine."

When the infant had calmed down, Melanie glanced up, and then flinched. Consumed by the task of comforting the baby, she'd temporarily forgotten about Luke. Her surprise turned to concern at the sight of his shocked expression. "Mr. Jackson," she asked, moving a step closer to him. "Are you all right?"

*   *   *

"Mr. Jackson?"

Although he heard Melanie Faraday's soft voice, he couldn't respond. It was all he could do to try to reconcile the scene in front of him—the very proper Miss Faraday cradling a Mexican infant in her arms. *Her* infant, according to the older woman standing next to her. And there was no mistaking the baby's heritage—her olive skin tone and tufts of thick black hair attested to it. There wasn't a trace of Melanie's fair coloring at all.

Luke looked from the infant to Melanie. Eyes as blue as a Texas summer sky stared right back at him. Wide, innocent eyes, surrounded by the longest eyelashes he'd ever seen. Her pale skin was nearly flawless, without a freckle or blemish in sight, nothing to suggest that she'd spent any time out in the hot Santa Fe sun without a bonnet or parasol. Pampered skin, befitting the daughter of a well-heeled businessman. At least that part of the scenario made sense.

Nothing else did.

"Flora," Melanie said in a kind but firm tone, one that denoted she was used to giving orders. She adjusted the brightly striped blanket around the baby's face. "Rosalita is asleep now." She handed the infant to the woman. "Please wait outside while I speak with Mr. Jackson."

"*Si, senorita.*" Flora carefully accepted the child, then turned on her heel and left.

The woman's departure snapped Luke back to attention. He glanced at the fan in his hand for a second before giving it back to Melanie. "You want to tell me what this is about, Miss Faraday? I wasn't told anything about there being a baby with you."

"I know, and I'm sorry about that."

"I think that's the first honest thing you've said to me."

A shadow passed over her eyes, making her appear young. As it was he guessed her to be about seventeen, nearly ten years younger than him.

"I've bungled this badly, I'm afraid." She twisted the remains of the fan in her gloved hands. "But there wasn't any other way." She met his gaze. "I have to get to Las Vegas."

He didn't miss the note of desperation in her voice. "Is that where your husband is?" he asked.

She shook her head, a thin tendril of curly blond hair escaping from her bonnet and falling against her cheek. "I'm not married."

An unwed mother. Understanding began to dawn. "Does your father know about the child?" he asked tightly.

"No, and he mustn't find out," she insisted. "He would be devastated to know I had done something like this." She sighed heavily. "There's a couple in Las Vegas who accept foundlings in their home. I just know they'll take little Rosalita in."

Luke's jaw clenched. This was more than he'd

bargained for, and much more than he wanted to deal with. A white woman with a Mexican child. One born out of wedlock. The whole situation repulsed him. He had to fight to keep the scorn from his voice. "And the baby's father?"

"Killed in the war," she said, a touch of sadness marking her words. "Her mother died three weeks ago."

Luke froze. "Her *mother?*"

"Yes," Melanie replied. "The birth was difficult—why are you staring at me like that?"

"I thought you were—"

"You thought I was what?" she asked, obviously perplexed.

He looked away. "I thought you were the baby's mother."

Melanie's face flushed crimson. "Why would you think that?"

"Because of what that woman said . . . and the way you handled the baby," he said, exasperated. "You calmed her down quickly. What else was I supposed to think?"

Melanie brought her hand up to the collar of her cloak and fidgeted with the dark green ribbon. Her cheeks were still pink. "I suppose I can see where you jumped to that conclusion," she said, averting her gaze for a brief moment. Then she looked back at him, determination evident in her eyes and in the high tilt of her chin. "But that's neither here nor there, Mr. Jackson. What matters is getting to Las Vegas. I believe we've wasted enough time already." She started to move past him, but he blocked her way.

"Hold on just a minute, Miss Faraday," he said, not bothering to disguise his irritation. Irritation that bordered on anger. "You're not going anywhere."

Melanie stilled at Luke's low, menacing tone. The stormy look in his eyes sent an icy chill down her spine, along with a flash of annoyance. "Mr. Jackson, I fully intend to go to Las Vegas, with or without your assistance."

"Of all the bull-headed . . ." he mumbled, then looked at her. "I don't understand any of this. First you deceive your father, and then you pull the wool over my commanding officer's eyes. I still can't figure how you did that one. All to take some Mexican kid to Las Vegas. Why you would even bother is beyond me."

Melanie gasped. "How can you say that?"

He shoved his hat back on his head and looked at her dead on. "I don't like being lied to, Miss Faraday. Not by anyone. And the soldiers of the American Army don't exist merely to be at your beck and call."

"I never thought—"

"I've spent the last year fighting Mexicans, defending our rights to live as free men in the Republic of Texas. That's what soldiers do—protect the rights of our citizens. Not import more Mexican *bambinos* into our country."

"Mr. Jackson—"

"I'm within my rights to turn around and walk out of here," he interrupted. "If I had a shred of sense I would do just that."

That did it. She didn't need this man's condescending attitude, or his callous disregard for an orphaned infant, not to mention his sanctimonious sermon. Gripping her fan, she barely felt the splintered wood pierce through her glove and into her skin. "I'll save you the trouble, *sir*," she said with derision. Then with a very unladylike shove, she burst past him and stormed out the door.

Flora stood a few feet from the hotel entrance, cradling a sleeping Rosalita. "Where is the American officer?" she asked in a hushed voice.

"He's decided not to join us," Melanie gritted out, still stinging from his tirade. "We'll be making the trip alone."

Her chaperone's coffee-colored eyes grew round. *"Senorita,"* she exclaimed loudly, despite the baby in her arms. "We can not go to Las Vegas alone. It is too dangerous!"

Rosalita began to stir in Flora's grasp. "We'll manage," Melanie said, with more courage than she felt. She tossed the remains of her fan in a nearby rubbish barrel, grimacing at the small blood spot on the palm of one glove.

Turning away from Flora she pulled a small piece of paper tucked in the cuff of her sleeve. The name Westbrooke was written on it, along with directions to Las Vegas. She knew in her heart she was supposed to take this trip.

She looked back at Flora. "We will pray for safety on our journey. We are doing the right thing, Flora. I know we are."

Flora shook her head. "You do not understand. The trail is very dangerous. Thieves, Indians, they all lay in wait to attack. And I have heard the weather can turn bad without warning."

"You forget that I've been on the trail before," Melanie replied calmly. Yet inside she was anything but collected. Yes, she'd traveled the Santa Fe Trail, but in the comfort of her father's plush coach, complete with luxurious amenities, along with being well guarded. Even then the journey had been long and difficult in some places. But they weren't traveling back to Missouri, only to Las Vegas. The town was merely a few days away.

"We'll be fine, Flora," she said, as much to convince herself as her chaperone. Melanie glanced down at Rosalita's cherubic face, and took the child from Flora. "I made a promise to her mother," she said, stroking the baby's petal-soft cheek, the infant's tiny eyes fluttering open. "I'll do everything in my power to honor it."

Still looking doubtful, Flora frowned. "I would feel much better if the officer was going with us."

"So would I," a male voice said.

Melanie jumped at the sound of Luke speaking behind her. She turned and faced him, hugging Rosalita to her breast. She shot him what she hoped was a bone-chilling look. To her consternation he seemed unfazed.

"You can't go to Las Vegas alone," he asserted. "It's too dangerous." He nodded at Flora. "Your friend is right, except for one thing."

"What's that?" she asked hotly, peeved that he'd heard their conversation. Exactly how long had he been standing behind her?

"I'm not an officer. And once I see you safely to Las Vegas, my duty is done." He stepped closer to her and peered down. "We have wasted enough time, and I have my orders. I gave my word to my superior that I would escort you, and I never go back on my word." A steely glint entered his eyes. "The sooner we leave, the quicker I can get back home to Texas."

And get rid of you, she could tell he wanted to add, but didn't. His animosity toward her was evident in his expression. "Fine," she said. "If we're stuck with each other, we might as well make quick work of it." She turned to Flora. "Gather the other children."

Luke's mouth dropped open. "What other children?"

"Rosalita's brothers." Melanie looked back at the tall soldier, gleaning a small measure of satisfaction at his shocked reaction. "Raul, Rodrigo, and Ramon. We certainly can't leave them behind," she said with an exaggerated, syrupy sweetness. "Now can we?"

Chapter Three

"**D**ear Lord, what have I gotten myself into?"

"What's that, Luke?" Stanley Gorder asked from behind the counter of Stillman's Mercantile.

"Nothing," Luke replied quietly. He watched as Melanie attempted to corral the three Montez brothers near the back of the small clapboard store. They seemed intent on touching every item in sight with their grubby hands. Unfortunately they ignored her protests. It didn't help that the young woman had only a rudimentary grasp of Spanish, and Flora was too busy in the corner feeding Rosalita to be of much help.

The whip-thin storekeeper cinched the belt of his white apron more tightly around his frame. He gave Melanie and the children a disparaging look. "If that gal can't get those kids under control, I'm going to have to throw them out," Stanley threatened. "I can't have them tearing up my store."

"Ramon, put that down!" Luke heard Melanie exclaim as the oldest boy picked up a pair of expensive calfskin gloves. Apparently he didn't understand English, because instead of following her command, he tossed the gloves over her head to his younger brother.

Melanie spun around, her skirt whirling around her ankles, and faced the other boy. "Rodrigo, bring those here right this minute. *Aqui . . .* um *. . . ahora!*

Rodrigo grinned, but held on to the gloves.

Melanie placed her fists on her slender waist. "You do as I say!" she snapped, her patience apparently evaporating. "Give those to me." Her eyes suddenly grew wide. "Raul, no!" She hurried to the other side of the store, Ramon and Rodrigo suddenly forgotten.

Raul, who couldn't have been older than four, thrust both his hands into a barrel of penny candy. He dropped fistfuls of the treats on the wood floor, scattering them everywhere.

"That's it!" Stanley started to move from behind the counter, but Luke held up his hand. "I'll take care of it," Luke said wearily. They hadn't even started on their journey and things were already going badly.

"I've seen those boys before," Stanley said.

"They prowl the streets at all times of the day, even during the night. Never seen hide nor hair of their parents." He tipped his head in Melanie's direction. "I don't know why that young woman is with them now, but trust me, you don't want to get involved in this."

"I'm already involved," Luke said over his shoulder as he made his way to the back of the mercantile.

"Atencion!" he barked, his voice booming through the store. He felt a glimmer of satisfaction when the boys froze in place. He turned to Ramon and Rodrigo. *"Usted pondrá esos guantes lejos. Aqui!"*

The boys immediately put the gloves back where they had found them. Then Luke walked over to little Raul. The young child looked up at him defiantly before tossing another handful of candy onto the floor.

Luke took off his hat and bent over until he and Raul were face to face. *"Escójalo arriba,"* Luke said, telling the boy to pick up the candy. His lowered his voice purposely, showing the young child he meant business.

Raul looked at the mess at his feet and shook his head. He stared Luke straight in the eye, his small dark eyebrows knitting together in determination. "No!" he yelled, balling up his fists. "No, no, no, no, NO!"

Taking a deep breath, Luke narrowed his gaze.

He wasn't about to be disregarded by some ill-mannered little scamp. In a low, growling voice he explained in Spanish exactly what he would do to the boy if he continued to defy him.

The color instantly drained from Raul's complexion. Before Luke could react, the little boy scrunched up his face and let out a scream that would make a coyote tuck tail and run.

"What on earth did you say to him?" Melanie cried as she rushed to Raul's side. She pulled him close and he buried his head in her skirts, his body shaking with sobs.

Bewildered by the boy's outburst, Luke took a step back. "I just told him to clean up the candy," he explained in his defense.

"He said he would spank him," Ramon piped up from behind. The child went and stood by Melanie and his youngest brother. Rodrigo followed closely behind. Ramon crossed his arms and looked accusingly at Luke. "He was gonna spank Raul until he turned black and blue."

Melanie looked aghast. "You threatened him?"

Luke ignored her comment, instead he was more than a little surprised that Ramon had deliberately acted as if he hadn't understood Melanie. "You speak English?" he asked him.

"*Si,*" Ramon replied. A rebellious expression similar to his brother's appeared on his face. "Rodrigo and I speak English. Raul only knows a little bit."

"You can't spank him," Melanie continued, her eyes flashing with anger at Luke. "You're not his father."

"Then his father should spank him," Stanley called out from behind the counter.

"His father is dead," Melanie shot back. "And so is their mother."

Raul's wails grew louder.

Luke brought his fingertips to the bridge of his nose. Closing his eyes briefly, he tried to gain his bearings. The challenges of the trail seemed insignificant compared to dealing with these children and their self-appointed savior.

He opened his eyes and looked at Melanie, her gaze shooting daggers at him while her hand gently stroked Raul's dark hair. He said a quick prayer for patience, and then took a deep breath.

"I want you to listen carefully," he said, directing his words to Melanie. "The journey to Las Vegas will be dangerous. The last thing we need is for these three to cause trouble."

He turned to Ramon and Rodrigo, who appeared unfazed now that they were over their initial shock of Luke bellowing at them. Raul turned his face and peeked from behind the folds of Melanie's dress. "If you do not behave, *los chicos,* I won't hesitate to discipline any of you. And if that means spanking—"

"Mr. Jackson!" Melanie interrupted, indignant.

Luke gave her a sharp glance, and continued addressing the children. "If that means spanking," he repeated, "I will do it. And I guarantee you it will hurt. *Comprende?*"

"*Si,*" Ramon said reluctantly. But angry embers of resentment burned in his dark brown eyes.

"*Bueno.*" Convinced that he now held sway over the boys, he stepped back, and took a long look at each one of them. Their coal black hair stuck out in tufts all over their heads, and the strands had an oily sheen to them. Their clothes were faded and torn in several places, and all three looked as if a stiff wind would knock their slight frames over.

Something unfamiliar tugged at Luke's heart, but he quickly ignored it. He'd seen unkempt children before. He'd even seen orphans before. A twinge prickled in his chest. He knew he probably had made many children fatherless during the course of the war.

Without thinking, he briefly rubbed his palm down the length of his thigh, the memory of the bullet piercing his leg and the Mexican soldier who had fired it still sharp in his mind. While Luke had survived the battle, he'd made sure the other soldier hadn't.

He gave his head a hard shake. He couldn't dwell on those things now. He wouldn't let what the war had cost him—and countless others—to fester in his mind.

"Here you go, boys."

Pulled from his thoughts, Luke glanced at Stanley Gorder. The storekeeper had quietly walked up behind him, and was now handing each Montez child a stick of peppermint candy. "I'm sorry, ma'am," he said to Melanie, a somber expression etched on his angular face. "I didn't realize they were orphans."

Melanie's ire seemed to diminish slightly as the boys eagerly grabbed their candy from Stanley. Within seconds they were crunching the sweet treat between their yellowed teeth. "It's all right, Mr. Gorder," she said, then nudged Raul forward slightly. "Tell Mr. Gorder thank you," she urged all three of the children.

"Gracias," Ramon and Rodrigo said around bites of peppermint.

"Raul?" she prompted.

"Gracias," he whispered shyly. All traces of his formerly strong-willed behavior were completely gone. The transformation stunned Luke. The child was the picture of innocence as he carefully licked his stick of candy.

Flora walked over to the quiet group with a content Rosalita nestled securely in her arms. Melanie whispered something in her ear, and the plump woman nodded. In Spanish Flora told the boys to follow her, and immediately they left the store.

"I asked them to wait outside," Melanie said, turning to Stanley. "I'm sorry for their behavior, Mr. Gorder. I will pay for anything they ruined."

"No harm done, ma'am," Stanley replied. "I'll just get a broom and clean the candy up. Then I'll start filling Mr. Jackson's order." He turned and headed to the back of the store.

Melanie looked at Luke. "May I please have a word with you, Mr. Jackson?" she asked stiffly. She quickly glanced at Stanley, who was approaching with a large push broom. "In private?"

Luke nodded, leading her to a secluded corner of the store. Once they were out of earshot of Stanley, she spoke. "I can't in good conscience allow you to threaten the boys, Mr. Jackson."

He bristled at her imperious tone. "That wasn't a threat, Miss Faraday. It was a promise."

"But they're innocent children!"

"They didn't look so innocent to me," he responded coolly. "Two of them were pretending they didn't understand you. One of them outright defied me. That's a far cry from innocent in my book."

"You don't understand . . . you haven't lived their life. Those children don't need punishment, they need nurturing. They need someone to love them." Her eyes misted over.

For the second time that morning, something moved inside Luke's soul. Again, he dismissed it, annoyed that he was letting three ragamuffin kids and a teary-eyed female get to him. The sooner he was done with this trip, the better.

"Miss Faraday, what those boys need is discipline. And I'm not afraid to give it to them, if they deserve it." He placed his hat on his head. "If you'll excuse me, I need to check with Stanley about those supplies. We should be getting on our way." Spinning on his heel, he headed for the front of the store when her mumbling almost halted him in his tracks.

"Stubborn, pig-headed mule."

He couldn't stop a smile from twitching on his lips. He didn't turn around, but instead continued to walk away. *I could say the same about you, little lady.*

Chapter Four

Luke slapped the reins against the oxen's flanks. Like a finely tuned army regiment they started forward in perfect unison. Although he was no expert on oxen, he could tell this was a well-broken team. *They ought to be, for what she paid for them.*

As they headed out from the center of town, Luke could hear loud voices in the wagon behind him. The covered farm wagon had cost less than the oxen, but it was still a pretty penny. He couldn't help but marvel at how easily she'd paid for everything—the team, their supplies, even extra ammunition for his Colt 45. He had his Army-issue musket with him too. He hoped he wouldn't need to use either weapon.

The sudden squalling of the baby reached his

ears, along with lightning fast Spanish and frantic English. It appeared Miss Melanie Faraday had her hands full settling the children in the back.

Luke shifted to a more comfortable position in the wagon seat. This entire situation didn't sit well with him at all. Four orphans, a lily-white rich girl, and her Mexican chaperone, all in a fired-up hurry to get to Las Vegas. Part of him was curious as to why.

But another part of him, the more sensible part, didn't want to know. It was better if he didn't get involved. His duty was simple. All he had to do was escort the women and children to Las Vegas. Their reasons for going there weren't important. Once that was done he could go home. Back to his farm and his family . . . back where he belonged.

After a while the commotion died down, and Luke appreciated the respite. The baby was quiet, and the boys were silent. Within seconds the front opening of the canvas parted. Melanie slipped out and rather ungracefully plopped onto the seat beside him.

"Finally!" she said, the word coming out on a puff of breath.

Out of the corner of his eye he watched her touch a wayward strand of blond hair. The curl that had been so springy before lay limp against her cheek. She tucked it beneath her green bonnet.

Almost as soon as Santa Fe was behind them, the trail became bumpy. More than once Luke felt himself lifted off the seat as the wheels rolled over dried mounds and ruts.

"Mercy!" Melanie gasped after one particular rut in the road bounced them hard.

"Maybe you should ride in the back," Luke said, maintaining a tight grip on the reins.

"I'd rather not do that. The children are all sleeping, and Flora needs to rest. I don't want to wake them." She let out a tired sigh. "It took so long to get them settled in."

He didn't reply. Minutes later they hit another bump. Her shoulder slammed against his upper arm. To her credit, she didn't cry out, but by the tiny groan she made, he suspected the forceful contact had hurt.

A soft breeze blew across them, giving slight relief to the heat of the day. When Luke breathed in the moving air, he inhaled her scent along with it. Instead of cloying perfume, she smelled clean and fresh and definitely feminine. A strange, yet not altogether unpleasant sensation twisted inside him.

Luke shifted in his seat again, and tilted the front of his hat off his forehead, focusing his mind on the trail ahead and off the woman sitting beside him. It wasn't long before she made that nearly impossible.

"Such beautiful scenery," she said, smoothing the folds of her light-green skirt across her lap. In the distance the top of the Sangre de Christo Mountains appeared to touch the puffy white clouds streaking across the pale blue sky. "It's so very different from back home."

She paused as if she were waiting for him to reply. When he didn't say anything, she continued, "I'm from Boston."

They jostled over several consecutive ruts. The scraping of the wagon's wheels against the divots in the trail was the only sound between them. After a long silence she spoke again. "Where are you from?"

He paused before answering, and considered ignoring her question. But the good manners his mother had instilled in him since he was a young boy precluded him from being that rude. "San Antonio."

"That's nice. I've never met anyone from California before."

"Texas," he corrected through gritted teeth as the wagon dipped into a deep rut. "San Antonio's in Texas."

"Oh. Well, I've never been that keen on geography. Mathematics and literature were always my strong suits in school. Why, my teacher always said that I should take the schoolteacher's test. But I'm not so sure if being a schoolteacher is what I want to do. It's a big decision, you know. And what if I fail the test? It would all be for naught. Then again I do love children, and I can see myself teaching them their letters and numbers. What do you think, Mr.—"

"Dang it all!" Luke jerked the reins to the right, trying to avoid a huge bump that appeared in the road. Her incessant chatter had distracted him, and now the two left wheels were going over the hump, causing the wagon to tilt.

Out of the corner of his eye he could see Melanie's arms flailing outward, grasping for purchase. She let out a small cry as she slid away from him. Although she wasn't in any danger, he quickly transferred the reins into his left hand and grabbed her around her slender waist, pulling her close to him. He held onto her that way until the wagon became upright again.

He tensed, half expecting to hear the children start crying again. The baby whimpered a few times, but other than that he didn't hear a sound. He stifled a sigh of relief.

He turned and looked at Melanie, realizing they were practically nose to nose. Her eyes were the clearest shade of blue he'd ever seen, framed by thick, light brown lashes. Her skin wasn't as flawless as he'd presumed. There was a faint sprinkling of freckles across the bridge of her small, pert nose. Out of nowhere the word *adorable* popped into his mind.

"Mr. Jackson . . . you may let go of me now."

"Sorry." He cleared his throat and dropped his arm from her waist, then scooted as far away from her as he could on the seat. Clutching the reins in both hands, he stared straight ahead, bewildered and annoyed with the path his thoughts had taken.

"Is the trail always this rough? I don't remember—"

"Yes, the trail is rough. I need to concentrate. All that yapping you're doing isn't helping."

"Yapping?"

"So you can either stay up here and hush, or go in the back with the others, I don't care. Whichever you do, just be *quiet* about it."

It didn't take her long to make up her mind.

"I'm sorry I bothered you," she said stiffly.

He cast a swift glance in her direction. The rosy blush on her cheeks coupled with the iciness of her look told him he'd spoken too harshly. Before he could apologize she shot out from the seat and climbed into the back of the wagon, the canvas flaps flopping shut behind her.

Silence filled her absence. It was what he wanted, wasn't it? Now he could concentrate on driving the team as they headed eastward to Pecos.

That is, if he could get the image of her hurt expression out of his mind.

"Dreadful man," Melanie muttered as she sat down on the floorboard of the wagon.

"Pardon, *senorita?*" Flora whispered from the other end. "Is everything all right?"

"*Si,*" Melanie responded, forcing a cheerful note

in her voice before telling another fib. "We're making good progress."

"Bueno."

In the dim light underneath the canvas, Melanie watched as Flora reached over and touched Rosalita's cheek, then lay back down. The boys were still asleep, and Melanie was thankful for it. She was tired to the bone, and knew she should follow Flora's lead and take the opportunity to have a nap. But she couldn't, not with everything that was on her mind, including the infuriating Mr. Luke Jackson.

He was rude beyond belief. At least he could have pretended to be interested in making conversation. The only reason she'd jabbered on like that was because he was so quiet. Besides, she wanted to get to know him, since they were going to be spending the next few days together. As things stood between them now, she didn't trust him, especially after seeing how he'd handled the children. He was gruff and insensitive. A brute if she'd ever met one.

So why was the tingle in her belly still there?

It had started when he'd curled his arm around her waist and pulled her close to him as she struggled to gain her balance on the buckboard seat. He smelled of leather and rawhide and something distinctly masculine, all of which sent her senses reeling. The dark, smoky brown of his eyes hid secrets, and her curiosity was aroused even more than before.

But he'd constructed a barrier between them right

away, one that she couldn't scale. She wasn't sure she even wanted to.

Sighing, she tried to stretch out in the cramped wagon. Between the children, Flora and the supplies, there wasn't much room, but it couldn't be helped. She'd spent nearly all of the money her father had left before he went to Albuquerque. She had to save some of it for the journey back to Santa Fe.

It was unbearably hot underneath the shelter of the arched canvas. Sweat pooled on her brow, and she patted it away with her handkerchief. She found herself wishing for the light breeze and stunning New Mexico scenery outside the confines of the wagon. But she'd melt in a puddle first before she'd sit next to The Grump again.

Her eyelids, gritty with dust, grew heavy. All she had to do was get the boys and the baby to Las Vegas, and to the Santa Anna orphanage. She'd keep that task in the forefront of her mind, and her thoughts away from Luke Jackson as much as possible.

Unfortunately, that was easier said than done.

Chapter Five

Melanie's eyes flew open as the wagon lurched to a stop. She rose from her reclining position, her limbs and back aching with stiffness. She didn't remember falling asleep.

The boys were already awake and scrambling to get out of the wagon. After being cooped up for several hours she couldn't blame them. Ramon had lifted up one flap at the back of the wagon when she laid her hand on his arm.

"Now, boys," she said. "I want you to behave yourselves, and to help Mr. Jackson any way you can."

"I don't think he likes us much," Ramon said sourly.

Her heart pinched at his truthful words. "Regardless, Ramon, we should still do our part. It will make the trip more pleasant . . . for all of us." She met each boy's gaze. "Please? *Por favor?*"

Ramon paused and looked at his two brothers. He said a few words in Spanish to Raul, who then frowned. After a moment however, Rodrigo and Raul both nodded and Ramon turned to Melanie. "*Si, senorita.* We will help Mr. Jackson. But only because you asked us to."

Her breath came out in a relieved rush. "*Gracias,* Ramon."

He lifted up the flaps and let the other boys climb out of the wagon first. Then he hesitated.

"Ramon?" Melanie picked up Rosalita. The baby was just now waking up. "Is something wrong?"

"I don't see why we have to go to Las Vegas."

She stroked Rosalita's soft scalp. "Because your new home is there."

He frowned.

"There's a wonderful couple there who is very kind." At least Melanie assumed they were. Anyone who would take orphans into their home had to have a kind heart. "I'm sure you'll like them. And you and your brothers and sister will have a roof over your heads and good food to eat. And there may be other children there to play with."

A shadow passed over his face. "I wish we could stay in Santa Fe. I wish we could stay with you."

Instinctively, Melanie drew Rosalita closer to her as a tightness squeezed at her throat. "Oh, Ramon," she said softly. "I wish you could too. But I simply can't take care of all of you. You need a mother and a father."

"But you're already taking care of us. You have since *Mama* died."

Inside she felt her heart crumbling. How could she explain to a young boy how complicated things were? That she couldn't simply adopt four children without being married first? Besides, she had the distinct feeling her fiancé wouldn't appreciate having orphaned Mexican children thrust upon him right after their wedding. "Ramon, I'm sorry, but this is the way it has to be."

He shot her a resentful look, and then leaped out of the wagon.

Melanie sat back and sighed.

"You care too much for them," Flora said from behind.

"*Si.* I can't help it." She planted a kiss on Rosalita's forehead.

The older woman moved closer to her. She seemed weary, even though she had slept most of the day. "Protect your feelings as best you can, *senorita.* It will be difficult enough when we get to Las Vegas."

"I know, I know." But Melanie knew it was too late. The children had already found their way inside her heart. When she left them in Las Vegas, she would leave a part of herself behind too.

* * *

Luke didn't hesitate giving the boys their orders in Spanish. "Rodrigo and Raul, you pick up kindling for the fire. There's lots of brush lying around here. Ramon you come with me, we'll water the team at the river."

To his surprise, all three boys obeyed without a word of protest. Yet he saw the sparks of resentment in Ramon's eyes as the young man fell in step beside him. But that was to be expected. It was clear the boy didn't want to be on this journey any more than he did.

After a fairly long walk they reached the banks of the Pecos River. Luke handed a jug to Ramon. "Fill that up," he said.

Ramon took it and moved a few feet away, dipping the narrow-mouthed container in the rushing water.

Luke surveyed the river as the oxen drank their fill. The water reached the very top of the bank. He was grateful for the clear sky above them. With the level this high, one strong rainstorm could easily cause a flood.

Kneeling upstream at the edge, Luke cupped his hands and scooped up the water, scrubbing the trail dust off his face. He rose, twinges of pain running through his thigh from sitting for so many hours steering the team. Soon Ramon returned with the full jug.

"Gracias," he said, taking the container. The boy simply nodded and looked at him defiantly, but

didn't say a word. Luke felt a bit of admiration toward him for keeping his emotions under control. He glanced down at the reins in his hand. Without hesitation he gave them to Ramon.

The surprise on Ramon's face was priceless. He stared at the reins as if unsure of what to do with them.

"Lead the team," Luke replied to Ramon's silent question. "When we get back to camp, tie them up near the grove of trees. They'll be fine there during the night."

"Si," was all Ramon said. But his squared shoulders and lifted chin spoke volumes. Luke himself felt a measure of satisfaction at pleasing the boy. The emotion caught him off guard, but it was nice.

When they arrived at the campsite Rodrigo and Raul had collected a good pile of twigs between them. Ramon split away from them and went to tie up the team. Melanie walked back and forth with Rosalita, whispering something in her ear. The baby cooed in reply, making Melanie laugh. An unexpected smile formed on Luke's lips at the sight.

Suddenly Ramon ran to them, waving his arm toward the grove of trees. *"Senorita! Senor* Jackson! It's Flora—she's sick. *Ella vomita!"*

"She's throwing up?" Luke's own stomach lurched.

"Si!"

Quickly Melanie thrust Rosalita at Luke. "I must see to her," she said.

He had no choice but to take the baby. "What am I supposed to do with this?" he asked, holding the bundle awkwardly.

But Melanie had already rushed off. "Talk to her," she called out over her shoulder.

Talk to her? He looked down upon Rosalita's chubby, peaceful face. Her eyes were black as coal, rimmed by a fringe of long dark eyelashes. They opened as he gazed at her, and he felt an odd yearning sensation deep inside him.

Then that peaceful face scrunched up into something resembling a lumpy potato. In the next second she let out a howl that nearly deafened him.

"Good Lord!" he said, flinching at the squall. When she continued to scream he started talking to her, first in English then in Spanish. "Good baby . . . nice baby . . ." That didn't work. A cold sweat broke out on his upper lip. "Okay, now what?"

Remembering how Melanie walked around with her, he began to pace back and forth in front of the wagon. On impulse he lightly patted her diapered bottom. Almost immediately she stopped crying.

He looked up and saw the boys playing some sort of game with the twigs. He started to chastise them, but kept quiet. He didn't want to disturb Rosalita, now that her eyelids were starting to close.

She was fast asleep in his arms when Melanie and

Flora returned. Flora leaned on Melanie as she guided her back to the wagon. Her normally tanned skin looked pale.

"I'll get her settled in," Melanie said. "Will you be all right for a few more minutes?"

He glanced down at Rosalita, still sleeping. "We'll be just fine."

Chapter Six

Melanie found cooking over an open fire to be a challenge, but one she was prepared to face. She made a simple stew of potatoes, carrots, and dried beef, along with biscuits which fortunately turned out fairly light and fluffy. Melanie took a bowl of the broth to the wagon where Flora was resting. She was gratified when the woman took a few sips of the hot liquid, all the while apologizing for being sick.

"Nonsense," Melanie said, smoothing the blanket over Flora's legs. The sun had nearly set and the air had turned chilly. "Just get some rest and don't fret about it."

"I am sure I'll feel better in the morning," Flora said weakly. She closed her eyes. "I am not used to traveling."

"None of us is," Melanie replied softly. "Except Mr. Jackson."

But Flora was already asleep.

As quietly as she could Melanie crept out of the wagon. She walked over to the campfire where Luke and the boys were sitting. The two older children were playing tic-tac-toe in the dirt, while Raul lined up several small stones he'd collected. Luke was holding Rosalita, who was awake and making sweet cooing noises.

Surveying the scene, Melanie felt an ache deep inside her soul. Would children be a part of her's and Ethan's future? Would her fiancé cradle their baby, just as Luke was cradling Rosalita? As hard as she tried, she couldn't imagine it.

"Boys, it's time for bed," she said, forcing herself to think of the present and not of her uncertain future. "Go quietly. Flora is sleeping."

The children stood up, not bothering to brush the dirt off their pants. Raul scooped up his treasures and stuffed them in his pocket and followed his brothers to the wagon. Melanie watched until all three were inside, then she went to Luke.

"I'll take her," she said, reaching for the baby. "She needs to be fed and changed. Then, hopefully, she'll fall asleep."

He looked up at Melanie. Was that reluctance she saw in his eyes? It was so fleeting, she wasn't sure.

His expression became blank and he handed Rosalita over to her. The baby began to whimper.

"There, there," Melanie whispered near her ear. "I know you're hungry." She turned and headed for the wagon.

"She likes to be patted," she heard Luke say behind her. "On her rump," he added quickly.

Melanie spun around. She almost grinned at the sight of Luke's reddened complexion.

"She seems to like that," he said, clearing his throat. He rose quickly and turned from her. He picked up a lantern and lit it. "I need to check on the team."

He walked away, leaving Melanie to yet again wonder at him. He was alternately the most intriguing and the most infuriating man she'd ever met.

An hour later, after the boys and Rosalita were asleep, Melanie grabbed her shawl and exited the wagon. After having slept a few hours during the day, she wasn't all that tired. The rich aroma of coffee filled her senses as she walked toward the fire.

"Want a cup?" Luke asked when she approached.

"Please." She sat down on an upside down crate. It wasn't comfortable, but it was preferable to the ground, which was where Luke was sitting. He didn't seem to mind, though. He poured the dark liquid into a tin cup and handed it to her.

"Thank you," she said, taking a sip. The strength

of the brew nearly knocked her off her seat, but she fought to maintain her composure. "Good," she said, only coughing once.

He drank down a big gulp without reaction.

They sat in silence for a short while. For once the quiet between them wasn't awkward. Melanie listened to the sounds of the night—a coyote howling in the distance, the crackling sound of the fire, the crickets chirping their evening songs. She looked around and noticed the stack of clean dishes near the fire. Apparently, while she had tended to the children and Flora, he had washed them with water from their drinking jug. She felt a small glimmer of appreciation at the gesture. It was one less task she had to deal with.

She tucked back a chunk of her wayward hair. She needed to pin it up, but didn't have the desire to. Out here in the wilderness, grooming was the least of her concerns. Tomorrow she would fix it properly.

"Nice night," Luke said, surprising her by being the first to break the silence.

"Yes," she replied, gathering her shawl closer to her. "A bit chilly, though."

"That's because of the mountains. Hot during the day, cool at night." He took another sip of his coffee.

"Is it the same in Las Vegas?"

"I suspect it is."

She looked at his profile as he stared at the fire. A

shadow of light brown whiskers had already formed on his upper lip and chin, adding to his already rugged exterior. He'd removed his hat, and she saw finger tracks where he'd ran his hand though his hair more than once. He was so different, both in appearance and demeanor, than any other man she knew. She thought back on their day together. Although he obviously resented her and the boys, he took his duty seriously, making sure that she and Flora and the children were taken care of. The least she could do is tell him the truth, and explain why they were here.

"I owe you an apology, Mr. Jackson," she said, gripping the warm coffee cup more tightly. "I should have been completely up front with you back in Santa Fe."

He quirked a brow but said nothing. It was as if he were waiting for her to continue.

"It's just that I didn't know what else to do. Caridad, the children's mother, died nearly three weeks ago. I've been caring for them, with the help of Flora. Before she died Caridad asked that I find a home for her sons and baby. She had no family nearby and no friends that could take them in."

"But why Las Vegas?"

"I made a few inquiries on behalf of Caridad." She set her cup down and rose from her seat. "The one charity house in town was full. I didn't know what I was going to do. Fortunately, as I was leaving the house, a man by the name of Mr. Denham approached me and told me about the Westbrookes. At that point I knew my prayers had been answered."

He considered her for a moment, doubt creeping in his eyes. "Let me get this straight. A complete stranger sees you coming out of a charity house, tells you that a couple you don't know in a town you've never been to, are willing to take in four orphaned Mexican children. And you believed him."

"Yes. I know it doesn't make much sense. But he was a very nice man, very dapper and articulate."

Luke rolled his eyes. "Oh, well then I'm sure he's the epitome of honesty."

His sarcasm stung. "You don't understand. I met Caridad only a few weeks ago. At that time she made tortillas at a small stall in the market. Even then when she was swollen with child and she looked so ill . . . I felt such . . . pity for her." Melanie swallowed the lump that had suddenly come to her throat. "But soon we became friends. I was there when Rosalita was born." She turned her back on Luke and the fire, the flames warming her body but not the coldness of the memory. "She begged me to look after her children. What else could I do but give her my word?"

"Why didn't you tell your father? A man as well connected as he is could have helped you."

"My father." She faced him. "I love him very

much, but he wouldn't understand. He's so caught up in this business venture of his. I knew bothering him with this would be pointless."

Luke frowned. "So instead you forged his name on a letter and constructed an elaborate ruse."

"I said I was sorry for that." Melanie looked away. "Why should I expect you to understand?"

He picked up his hat and slowly stood. Melanie saw him wince, and she was reminded of his injury. "Does it hurt badly?"

"What?"

"Your leg."

He glanced down. "At times. But it's healing." He stepped toward her, limping slightly. His gaze connected with hers. "I understand more than you think, Miss Faraday. I'm not in your shoes, so it's not my place to judge you or your actions. You're doing what you think is best. I hope it all works out for them . . . and for you." He tossed the remains of his coffee on the fire and set the cup on the ground. "I'm turning in. Good night."

"Good night." Melanie watched as he ambled over to the wagon and spread his bedroll underneath. Without a word of complaint he slid inside it.

She felt guilty that he had to sleep underneath the wagon, but it would have been improper for him to sleep inside, even chaperoned. More and more she was coming to realize he was a true gentleman. She never would have believed that as little as a day ago.

The fire was almost embers by now. As quietly as she could she tiptoed to the wagon so as not to disturb anyone. But as she climbed in her foot slipped and she fell backward on the ground, landing on her backside.

"Oof," she said, then clamped her hand over her mouth.

"Are you okay?"

She looked up and saw Luke standing over her. He reached out his hand and helped her up, gently gripping her by the elbow.

"I'm fine," she said, her face heating up with embarrassment. "Just clumsy."

"You're not clumsy. It's dark out here. Let me help you."

He placed his hands on her waist and lifted her up with ease. Although she had a good grip on the end of the wagon, his hands lingered, sending trickles of warmth down her spine. "Thank you," she said, when he finally let go.

"Your welcome." He took a step back as she climbed in. She gave him one last glance before letting the canvas flap fall.

Searching for a bare spot in the wagon bed, she maneuvered around children and supplies until she found one. Removing the pins from her hair, she let it fall down her back, not bothering to braid it. Lying down, she closed her eyes, the memory of Luke

Jackson's strong hands on her waist following her into sleep.

Melanie was jolted awake by the loudest crash of thunder she'd ever heard. Immediately everyone in the wagon was sitting upright, while Rosalita started to cry.

"*Dios mio!*" Flora said. "What was that?"

"Thunder," Melanie said.

"It sounded more like the sky was falling." As if on cue another boom rocked the wagon, followed closely by a flash of lightning. The boys huddled together, and Raul began to cry.

"He's scared," Ramon said, his own voice sounding shaky.

"There's nothing to be afraid of." Melanie picked up the baby. "Raul, come here."

He scooted over to her and she put her arm around his shoulders. "It's just thunder and a little lightning. I know the sounds are scary, but they can't hurt us." She gave each of the boys an encouraging smile.

Within minutes heavy raindrops plopped on the canvas covering, their sound echoing through the wagon. It didn't take long for the singular drops to turn into a downpour. The canvas sagged in spots where the water weighed it down. Thunder and lightning continued to crash and crackle. She wondered with a pang of alarm how Luke was faring out in the storm.

The flaps suddenly opened and he popped his head inside. "A bit wet out here," he quipped, water dripping from the brim of his hat. Without hesitation he climbed inside.

"Boys, climb to the other side of the wagon," Melanie said. "Over by Flora. Move some of the supplies around so Mr. Jackson will have some room."

After moving and switching things and people around, Melanie and Luke ended up sitting side by side. He was soaked clear through. "I'm getting your dress wet," he said as their shoulders touched.

"That's alright." But she knew he couldn't spend the rest of the night in wet clothes. Cradling Rosalita in her left arm, she reached for a blanket. "Take off your shirt and wrap yourself in this."

"I'll be fine," he said, waving her off. "I've survived worse conditions than a storm."

"What if you catch a cold?" she asked, trying to appeal to his practical side. "We already have one ill person, we don't need two."

Wordlessly he took the blanket from her and stripped off the dripping shirt, then wrapped the coarse material around his shoulders. Wearily he leaned his back against the raised wooden side of the wagon.

Before long, the thunder and lightning ceased. The rain continued to pour, its cadence steady and rhythmic. The sound put the boys and Flora to sleep, and eventually Luke. Melanie changed and fed Rosalita. Soon the baby was also sleeping.

By this time Melanie was too unnerved to go back to sleep. The excitement of the storm, the closeness of Luke . . . she could practically feel his warmth radiating, even though they weren't touching. She sighed, bringing her own blanket up to her chin, trying to calm her jittery thoughts.

Sleep would be a long time coming tonight.

Chapter Seven

When Luke awoke the next morning, he sensed an unfamiliar pressure against his shoulder. He looked down. Melanie was leaning against him, her mouth slightly open and her eyes closed. Her breathing was deep and steady. She was sound asleep.

During the night the blanket had slipped from around him, and her cheek was resting on his bare skin. He started to wake her up, but decided against it. She looked settled and tranquil, and he didn't want to disturb her sleep. A quick glance around the rest of the wagon told him everyone else was asleep too.

He closed his eyes briefly, trying not to think about the woman next to him, but unable to get her off his mind. The rain continued to hammer down outside, thumping off the waterproof canvas. He thought about what she'd told him last night. The plight of the children along with her dilemma had touched something inside him that he didn't want to contemplate. He wished she hadn't said anything. It was easier to keep an emotional distance when he hadn't known the true purpose of the trip.

"Senor?"

He looked up and saw Raul crawling over his brothers and coming toward him. He had a pinched look on his face. "I have to go to the privy," he said in Spanish.

Luke sighed. He now knew from experience that once a child had to go, he had to go immediately. "I'll wake *senorita* Faraday."

"I want you to take me."

"You do?"

The little boy nodded.

Luke scrubbed a hand over his face. "Alright." He nudged Melanie. "Miss Faraday."

"Hmmm?" she said, nuzzling her cheek against his shoulder. Her eyes then flew wide open and she jerked away from him. "Oh! I-I'm so sorry."

He had to fight the urge to smile at her flustering. "Raul needs to take care of business."

Sitting up, she flung off the blanket. "Of course. I'll take him right away."

"He wants me to."

She looked at him. "He does?"

"Yep."

When she turned to Raul he nodded, the impatience on his face increasing. Luke figured they better hurry. He reached for his damp shirt and slid it over his body, flinching at the coldness of the fabric. "We'll be right back."

"Thank you for doing this."

He looked at her for a moment. They were close enough that he could see the drowsiness in her eyes and the mark on her cheek where she had laid against him. Her hair was unbound and tumbling over her shoulders like a curtain of blond silk. His fingers tingled at the thought of touching a strand of it.

"Senor . . . por favor!"

He turned to Raul who looked about to burst. *"Vayamos,"* he said, opening up the flaps.

Luke looked through the opening and groaned at what he saw.

The thunderstorm had indeed caused the Pecos River to flood its banks. Jumping down from the wagon, Luke landed in water up to his ankles. He hauled Raul out and set him down. The boy darted for the nearest tree.

Luke shoved his hand through his wet hair, giving the ends a hard yank. The wagon wheels were stuck in mud and water up to the spokes. His plans for hitting the trail by noon disappeared into thin air.

They weren't leaving anytime soon.

He saw Raul struggling to walk through the flood as he tried to reach the tree. Picking up the boy, Luke carried him to the other side of the wagon. "No one will see you here," he assured Raul.

After Raul had finished his business and Luke had done the same, they went back to the wagon. He grimaced. At least one whole day lost, if not more. A seed of frustration took root inside him.

It sprouted tenfold at the chaos in the wagon.

Ramon and Rodrigo were bickering over a pair of brown socks with holes in them. Rosalita was crying—actually shrieking was more like it. Flora, apparently still under the weather, was resting in a back corner of the wagon, staying out of the fray. Melanie was attempting to referee the boys while she unfolded one of the baby's diapers. His head pounded from the noise.

When he helped Raul into the wagon, Melanie's attention turned to Luke. "I thought we could eat breakfast on the trail," she said, picking up a squalling Rosalita, apparently immune to the racket. "We have a few biscuits left from last night and some dried meat."

He remained standing in the rain. "We're not going anywhere," he said in a low voice.

"We're not?"

The boys arguing increased. Now Raul had joined in the verbal battle.

"The land's flooded. The wagon's stuck," Luke said, raising his voice to be heard over the ruckus.

"What?" Melanie yelled back.

Luke's anger simmered under the surface. "Enough!" he shouted, effectively quieting down everyone but Rosalita. He pointed at the baby. "Do something with her!"

"I am," Melanie shot back. "She's wet and hungry. I'm changing her as fast as I can. There's no need to be so grouchy about it."

"Oh, I have a right to be grouchy," he said in a menacing tone. "Being stuck here with four brats and a woman without a lick of commonsense gives me that right." He yanked the flaps shut and stalked away from the wagon, ruing the moment he met Melanie Faraday.

"What's a brat?" Ramon asked after Luke had stormed off.

Melanie continued diapering Rosalita. "A child," she said without looking at him. She couldn't possibly tell him and his brothers the true meaning of the word. In fact she was thinking *brat* would be more appropriately applied to Luke Jackson.

She tied together two diaper corners, fuming inside. Every kind word and thought she'd ever had about the man disintegrated. "Ramon, you and Rodrigo find some dry clothes for Raul," she instructed.

While the boys searched the wagon for a shirt and trousers, Melanie picked up the baby. "Horrible, beastly man," she muttered under her breath.

Out of the corner of her eye she saw Flora hold out her arms. "Here, let me take her," she said, offering to accept Rosalita.

"Did you hear what he called them?" Melanie refused to relinquish her hold.

"Si, senorita."

Melanie glanced at the boys and lowered her voice. "Do you know what it means?"

Flora nodded. "But he is upset, as he should be. We are stuck here. I think he is not used to children and babies. Most men cannot take the noise."

Sitting back on her knees, Melanie blew a limp lock of hair from her forehead. "I see your point," she agreed. "Still, that gave him no right to say mean things about the children." *Or about me.* Her pride was more than a little pricked by his disparaging remarks about her commonsense. Or lack thereof, in his rotten opinion.

She looked at Flora, who still seemed ready to take Rosalita. "I'm sorry," Melanie said. "I got so upset I forgot to ask you how you're feeling."

"Better," she said, smiling a little and taking the baby from her. "I still do not like the bumpy road."

"Oh, Flora." Melanie held her head in her hands. "I shouldn't have dragged you all the way out here."

"No, *senorita*. It is fine. I am sure I will get used

to it." She cradled Rosalita. "I will feed her, if you like."

For the next few hours, the six of them stayed in the back of the wagon as the rain continued to fall. It didn't take long for the boys to get restless, so Melanie played word games with them and told stories from her childhood while Flora kept Rosalita entertained. The entire time she expected Luke to return, but he never did. But she refused to worry about him. He was a grown man and could take care of himself. Besides, where would he go? They were all stuck here.

Around mid-afternoon the rain finally let up. Eager to get out of the wagon, the boys barreled through the opening, landing on the ground with a splash of water and mud. They ran around the waterlogged field as if they were caged animals suddenly set free.

Melanie stayed behind and held Rosalita while Flora climbed out of the wagon. Then Melanie stepped down, her feet threatening to slide out from under her in the slippery mud. That was all she needed, to land backside first on the ground like she did the night before.

She looked at the sunken wagon wheels, her heart plummeting at the sight. They were definitely stuck. No wonder Luke was so upset. She glanced down and saw his blanket and bedroll sucked into the ground. It was difficult to tell where the mud ended and his makeshift bed began.

Slogging through the water and muck she reached the front of the wagon. The sun was high in the sky, shining brightly as if a drop of water had never hit the ground. Shading her eyes, Melanie looked toward the grove for signs of Luke. Not only did she not see him, but the oxen were missing too.

Panic welled up inside her. Hiking up her skirt, she hurried to Flora. "Have you seen Mr. Jackson?"

"No, *senorita*. He is not here?"

Melanie surveyed the area again. He wouldn't leave them stranded, would he? "I'm sure he's at the river with the team," she said, trying to convince herself as much as Flora. Yet she couldn't release the niggling thought that he might have abandoned them. "I'm going to look for him."

Flora's thin black brows lifted. "Maybe you should wait until he comes back."

"It will only take a minute," she said, already binding up her skirt in her fists.

"What about the boys?"

Melanie looked at them. They were having a grand time, throwing balls of mud at each other. They were also covered in the stuff from head to toe. "Just let them play," she said. "They can take a bath later."

Remembering the direction Ramon and Luke had

headed out the day before, she followed in their footsteps. When she reached the river Luke wasn't there. Examining the moist ground, she saw a man's boot print, along with several animal hoof marks. Knowing they had to belong to Luke and the oxen, she decided to follow them.

The tracks diverged from the river and headed toward the mountains. The sun's heat began to beat mercilessly on her head, and she wished she'd thought to take her bonnet. The air was sticky and muggy. Wiping the sweat from her eyes, she continued onward.

But she didn't find Luke or the team, and the tracks became smeared and hard to follow. She walked and walked and walked, until the daylight began to fade and she was forced to turn around and head back.

Even though she thought she was backtracking the way she came, she still didn't see the river. By the time she realized there were more than one set of tracks she was thoroughly disoriented. All she saw was a vast field of mud, dotted with a few trees. Bile climbed up her throat at the reality of her situation. How had she become so lost?

Her feet sore and tired, she stopped walking. Tears streamed down her cheeks and she sank to the ground, not caring that the mud and water seeped through her dress. Luke was right. She didn't have any commonsense. Apparently she lacked a sense of direction too. Defeat washed over her, just as the rain had washed over the land. She should have never come here, should have never brought four innocent children and her companion into her scheme. Whatever happened to them would be her fault. Letting her face drop into her hands, she whispered thickly, "I'm sorry."

Chapter Eight

Luke led the team back to the campsite from the Pecos River. He'd spent the morning and most of the afternoon there, taking semi-shelter under a tree as the oxen drank and wandered around the surrounding area. When the sun had emerged he had joined them, leading the team toward the mountains. The animals had seemed restless because of the storm, and he had his own dissatisfaction to work off. His clothes and skin were drenched, and he welcomed the sun's warmth.

He realized things also seemed a little clearer in the bright light of the day.

He knew he had to apologize to Melanie. He'd insulted her and the children, and that was uncalled for. It was also uncharacteristic of him. Normally he didn't lose his temper. Keeping a firm rein on his feelings had saved his life more than once during battle. But there was something about this situation, and about Melanie in particular, that knocked his emotions off balance.

He nudged the oxen along, formulating his apology in his mind. When he reached the camp he almost dropped the reins.

"What's going on here?" he asked, bewildered by the sight of three boys practically entombed in mud. Even now they continued to throw the thick brown slime at each other, laughing as handful after handful hit their bodies with loud splats.

Luke couldn't help but crack a small smile. When he was younger he and his brothers would have had a mud fight too under the same circumstances. He shook his head and led the team to the grove, surprised that Melanie had allowed the Montez brothers to get so filthy.

After securing the team he headed back to camp. He reached the back of the wagon when Flora poked her head outside the canvas flaps. "*Senor* Jackson, you have returned." She started to descend from the wagon. "I have just laid Rosalita down for her nap."

Luke quickly moved to help Flora down.

"*Gracias,*" she said, smoothing her hair back in its tight black bun. Thin slivers of silver threaded through the dark strands and glinted in the sunlight.

"Where is Miss Faraday?" he asked.

Flora stopped smoothing her hair. "She is not with you?"

"No. Why would she be?"

"She went looking for you," Flora said, a note of panic entering her voice. "She has been gone quite a while . . . I thought she had found you."

He muttered an oath under his breath. "Now why would she go and do a fool thing like that for?" Flora opened her mouth to speak, but Luke silenced her with his hand. "Never mind. Who knows why she does half the things she does? And it always seems to make more work for me." He moved away from the wagon. "I'll go look for her. You keep an eye on the children."

"Si." Flora's expression filled with worry. "Hurry, *Senor* Jackson. If she is lost—"

Struggling to keep the aggravation from his voice he said, "I'll find her." He gave Flora a reassuring look and softened his tone. "Don't worry, she couldn't have gone far."

His hand went to his holster as he started for the river. He'd taken his pistol with him when he'd left camp earlier that morning, having learned from his time in the Army to always be prepared. Although they appeared to be the only travelers on this stretch of the trail, he didn't want to be caught off his guard.

When he arrived at the Pecos River he traveled up and down its banks, calling out Melanie's name and fully expecting her to reply immediately.

She didn't.

For a long while he kept calling, but there was no sign of her anywhere. He scanned the area around him. She could have gone off in any direction. Tension clawed at his neck and shoulders as the first impressions of anxiety came over him, replacing his previous irritation.

One thing was obvious—he wouldn't find her just by standing on the edge of the Pecos River. Taking a guess, he headed south from the bank, praying he would come across anything that would indicate where she might be.

He moved stealthily, having tracked down more than one stray lamb working on the farm back home. The sun was now hovering over the horizon, and Luke muttered a few more choice words. What if he didn't find her before dark?

Then he heard it, a sound so faint it just about escaped him. *Crying.* He spun in the direction of the weeping and tramped through the still-soggy ground. "Melanie?" he shouted.

"Luke?"

A tender sensation traveled through him at the sound of her calling out his name. Relieved, he ran to her. She was sitting on the ground, her dress wet and mud-spattered. He crouched down next to her, his aggravation and anxiety instantly dissipating at the distress he saw on her face.

"I got lost," she sobbed, looking up at him. "You were right. I don't have any commonsense. I'm too impulsive." As if to prove her words were true she reached up and unexpectedly grasped his shirt with both hands.

It seemed only natural to put his arms around her. The tension ebbed from his shoulders as he awkwardly ran his hand down her damp back. He recognized her tears for what they were. Not a sign of weakness, but an indication of her fear. During the past three years he'd seen mighty, stalwart men blubber like babies after facing a terrifying situation.

He'd also been known to shed a few tears himself.

"It's all right," he said quietly. "You're safe now."

"Because of you." She looked up at him, moisture shimmering on her cheeks. "I feel like an idiot, leaving camp like that."

"Then why did you?"

"I'd thought you'd left us."

"Left you?" He held her from him, stunned. "Whatever gave you that idea?"

"This morning . . . you were so angry at me . . . at the children." She sniffed. "Then you were gone for so long . . ."

"I know. I shouldn't have lost my temper."

"But we're stuck here, and it's my fault. I don't blame you one bit for being angry."

"You didn't cause the storm," he pointed out, feeling the need to comfort her, despite her echoing his own thoughts from the past several hours. Still, he wanted to relieve her of the guilt she kept piling on herself. He didn't like seeing her dejected like this. "As for me going home, Miss Faraday, I'll get there eventually."

She gazed up at him, her blue eyes bright with hope. "So you're not mad anymore?"

He shook his head and spoke the truth. "No, I'm not mad." He released his arms from her side and stood, then helped her up. "Let's go back to camp. Flora's worried about you."

She managed a watery smile. Taking a limp handkerchief out of the pocket of her dress she wiped her nose. A dark brown smear of mud stained the pale fabric when she drew it away from her face. Her smile changed into a frown. "I must look a fright," she said, looking down at her messy clothes.

He shook his head. "Not compared to the boys."

Her mouth formed a small o. "That's right. When I left they were playing in the mud." She grimaced. "How bad are they?"

A chuckle escaped him when they started back to their campsite. "I'll let you find out for yourself."

When they arrived at the camp, Melanie looked

sufficiently shocked. Flora and the boys were seated around the campfire, dipping their biscuits into their bowls, which were filled with stew. The mud had dried into hard patches on their bodies, and their clothes were stiff and brittle when they moved. They looked like they'd been dunked into a mud pit several times.

Turning her head at the sound of Luke's and Melanie's approach, Flora jumped up from her seat. "Oh, *senorita, senor!* I am so happy you are back!"

"Me too," Melanie said, greeting the woman with a hug.

"I was so worried, but I knew *Senor* Jackson would find you."

"He certainly did," she said. The sweet look Melanie gave him made his toes curl inside his boots.

"Do you want to eat?" Flora asked. "The boys were *muy* hungry, so when Rosalita fell asleep I fixed them something to eat."

"I'll have to eat later," Melanie said, giving each boy a hard look. "The children need a bath right away."

Ramon's, Rodrigo's and Raul's eyes grew round, the dried mud cracking around their cheeks.

"*Pronto,*" Luke said, sensing their protests before they said a word.

"But it's too dark," Ramon exclaimed.

"There's plenty of daylight left. And we'll take a

lantern with us." He turned to Melanie. "As soon as they're done eating their grub, I'll take them to the river."

"Are you sure?"

He could see fatigue pulling at the corners of her eyes. He nodded. "I'll need some clean clothes for them."

Melanie started for the wagon. "I'll be right back."

An hour later they all returned from the river, their skin and clothes freshly scrubbed, including Luke's. Ramon held the lantern and led the way to the campsite while Luke carried their wrung out, clean clothes in a burlap sack.

Melanie met them at the edge of the campsite and hurried the boys off to bed in the wagon. She accepted the sack from Luke and asked, "Where should I hang these up to dry?"

He noticed in the muted light of the lantern she still seemed tired, but she'd cleaned up a little. Well, really more than a little. Her hair was twisted back in a neat arrangement at the nape of her neck, and her face and dress were spotlessly clean. She smelled good too, like a field of wildflowers. The scent wasn't overpowering. He appreciated that.

He glanced around the campsite. "I'll rig up some sort of clothesline near the fire. The clothes will dry faster there."

"While you do that I'll go check on the boys. I don't want them waking up Rosalita."

Twenty minutes later the clothesline was ready. Fatigue was starting to set in on him too. He sat down and noticed a pot of coffee had already been brewed. Pouring himself a cup, he took a sip of the piping hot liquid. It wasn't as strong as he liked, but it was passable. For once he was glad he didn't have to brew it himself.

The sound of soft footfalls drew his attention away from his drink. He looked up to see Flora approaching from the wagon. "Where's Melanie?" he asked the older woman in Spanish.

"She was very tired, so I made her lie down. I told her I would take care of the clothes." Flora picked up the bag, walked over to the clothesline, then began draping the boys' clothing over the thin length of rope.

"While you were gone I had the boys help me move some supplies out of the wagon," she said. "There is room for you to sleep inside tonight."

He took a gulp of his drink. "*Gracias,*" he said, grateful for her thoughtfulness. He hadn't relished the thought of sitting up and sleeping again, or worse, sleeping on the muddy ground.

He heard her take a deep breath. "*Senor* Jackson, please don't be too hard on *Senorita* Faraday. She may not make the best decisions, but her heart is in the right place." She turned and faced him, holding one of the boy's trousers in her hand. "She cares about the children. Very much."

"I know. And if it makes you feel any better, I realize I have been too harsh with her." He stared off into the dusky distance, the outline of the mountains a pale shadow against the velvet sky. "There are enough perils on this trip. We don't need the added aggravation of being angry at each other."

Flora hung up the last piece of clothing. "You're right."

Luke looked at her. In a way she reminded him of his mother. They were both about the same age, and had the same air of calm wisdom about them.

"It's been a long day," Flora said, bringing him out of his thoughts. "I'm ready for bed. Good night. You should get some sleep too."

"I'll be there in a minute."

"Try not to wake the baby," she admonished lightly.

"Heaven forbid."

Flora smiled, then made her way to the wagon. After she'd left, Luke stared at the fire. An intense feeling of homesickness came over him. More than anything he just wanted to go home, to be back in San Antonio and his family's ranch. He wondered how his little brother Joshua was coping, having been left behind to take care of their mother and the ranch at the young age of fourteen.

But despite that, in the far recesses of his soul he felt a tinge of sadness at the thought of leaving

Melanie, Flora and the children behind. The sensation baffled him.

When had they managed to wriggle their way inside his heart?

Chapter Nine

The next morning Melanie awoke inside an empty wagon. It took a moment for her mind to register that she was alone, but there was no mistaking the emptiness surrounding her. She had room to stretch, to crawl, even to stand up if she ducked her head a little. According to the amount of daylight illuminating the inside of the wagon, she realized it was well into the morning.

Hurriedly she pinned up her hair and buttoned up her shoes. Climbing out of the wagon, she inhaled the scent of frying bacon, and saw Luke crouching near the skillet suspended over the fire. She hastened over to him.

"What are you doing?" she asked.

"Fixing breakfast." He speared a sizzling slab of bacon and turned it over with his fork.

"Where's Flora?"

"She and Rosalita and the boys took a walk. Probably out stomping wildflowers, knowing those three. They ate earlier."

Melanie touched her sleek hair with the palm of her hand. "Then why didn't you wake me? I would have made breakfast."

He looked at her, the corner of his mouth twitching. "I tried."

"You did?"

"Yep. But you wouldn't wake up. So we figured you needed your sleep." He turned his attention back to the fry pan.

Melanie was astonished. Sure she'd been tired last night. If truth be told she'd been more than tired. Exhausted, drained and weary, all rolled into one. She didn't remember anything once her head hit her folded blanket, which turned out to be a poor substitute for a pillow. Although the thought of Luke spending another night inside the wagon with them made her a bit apprehensive, apparently it was not enough to keep her from sleeping. She hadn't heard him coming in or going out. She hadn't heard anybody else, for that matter.

"How many?"

"What?"

"Bacon. How many pieces do you want??"

"Two," she mumbled, amazed by his ease with cooking. Her father could barely butter his toast by himself. Back in Boston a servant had always made their meals, or on rare occasions her mother would prepare a special dessert. Melanie had taken over the cooking and household duties after her mother's death, simply to have something to do to keep from wallowing in her grief.

But Luke was cooking as if he'd been doing it all his life.

The rest of the group came back just as Luke was dishing out breakfast. The bacon was crunchy but not blackened, and the biscuits perfect. It was a most delicious breakfast, tasting even better since she didn't have to prepare it herself.

After she finished every bite, she dabbed at her lips with her handkerchief. The sun shone brightly in the blue sky, and though there were clouds scattered above, they were light and fluffy, not dark and threatening. The ground around them was partially dry. "Do you think we'll be able to leave today?"

"I'd rather not risk it," he said around a mouthful of food. He swallowed before speaking again. "Even if we could get the wagon out of the mud, I'm afraid we might get stuck again."

"Oh," she said, disappointment knifing through her. She braced herself, knowing how angry Luke must be with her that their travel was delayed another day.

But he said nothing, merely finished his breakfast in silence. "I'm going to check on the team," he said, rising from his seat. "Would you mind doing the dishes?"

She blinked. Was this the same man who only yesterday morning called the children brats? Who since the moment they met acted as if she was a queen-sized thorn in his side? She could hardly reconcile him with the solicitous, not to mention excellent cook walking away from her now.

Whatever had caused the change she wasn't going to question, merely accept it gratefully.

While she washed the dishes the children returned with Flora. The boys played with each other in the open field next to the campsite, while Melanie entertained Rosalita and Flora tidied the inside of the wagon. Luke kept himself busy and out of sight. The morning went by quickly and peacefully.

At noon they lunched on biscuits and dried meat. To be honest, Melanie was growing tired of biscuits all the time, but no one else complained. The boys gobbled them up as if they were eating their last meal. She realized that the meals they'd been consuming on the trip, although simple and sparse, were more than what they had eaten at home and on the streets of Santa Fe. She ate every last crumb of her biscuit.

Flora took Rosalita back to the wagon for her nap while the boys walked a few paces from camp, then lay down on the ground and stared up at the sky. They pointed at the big fluffy clouds and jabbered to each other in Spanish.

Melanie and Luke remained by the fire. Luke picked up a stick and began doodling in the dirt. Melanie brushed imaginary fluff off the front of her dress, wishing she'd brought her needle work or a book with her on the trip to keep her occupied. But she hadn't expected there to be this much of a lull in their journey.

Luke looked up from his crude drawing. "Do you know how to shoot a gun?"

Surprise coursed through her at his question. "No."

He nodded slowly, as if contemplating something. Finally he said, "I think you should learn."

"Oh, I don't think that's necessary, Mr. Jackson."

"I do. What if something were to happen to me?"

Another wave of alarm crashed against her. She couldn't fathom the idea of his getting hurt . . . or worse. "Nothing will happen to you," she said brightly, as if voicing the words in as cheerful a tone as possible would make them absolutely true.

"We have to consider the possibility. How would you defend yourself?"

"Flora and I would manage."

He rubbed his chin. She heard the rough scrape of his fingers against his whiskers. "I'd feel a lot better if you knew how to fire a gun. Or at least my pistol."

"Your pistol?" Melanie suddenly felt nauseous.

"There's nothing to it, actually. Lots of women back home know how to use firearms." He turned somber. "After the Alamo, they had to learn. Many of them lost their husbands and sons there. It was up to them to protect their land and property."

She swallowed. She was unable to pinpoint why the idea of firing a gun frightened her so. Maybe it was the thought of holding an instrument of death in her hand. Those women were much braver than she could ever be.

He got to his feet and wiped the dust from his trousers. He took his military hat out of his pocket and placed it on his head, then started walking away.

"Where are you going?"

"To tell Flora to watch the boys. You and I are going to have some target practice."

"I'm still not sure about this, Mr. Jackson," Melanie said as they walked to the grove of trees.

That was plain obvious to Luke. Her complexion looked as white as the back of a bunny's cotton tail. Still, she needed to learn how to do this, and he had the time to teach her. There was no telling what kind of danger they would run into farther up the trail, and he wanted to make sure she would be prepared.

He halted several yards from the largest tree. Turning to her, he withdrew his Colt from its holster, and showed her the different parts of the gun. Then he held it out to her.

She stared at it, her eyes growing wide. She closed them for a moment, as if she had to convince herself to take it. Then she opened her eyes and grasped the handle of the gun.

"There," he said. "The first step is over."

Her hand holding the gun trembled slightly. "Now what?" she asked in a quivery voice.

"You have to learn to aim it."

"Like this?" She pointed the barrel straight at his chest.

His heartbeat jumped off track at the sight of the gun aimed at him. Carefully he guided the weapon away. "Yes, but watch where you're pointing that thing."

Her face reddened as she realized what she had done. "I'm sorry," she breathed, the gun shaking even more in her hand. "I could have killed you."

"Nah. It's not loaded."

She froze. "It isn't?"

"I wouldn't hand you a loaded gun, Miss Faraday, until I taught you how to use it. Your first lesson is to point the barrel at the ground when you're not shooting."

She immediately did as he told her. He took the gun from her and showed her how to aim, cock back the hammer, and pull the trigger. Soon he noticed she began to watch him with interest. When he finished with his instructions he handed the weapon to her and told her to practice aiming at the trees. This time she took it without hesitation.

After she'd practiced a while aiming and firing the empty pistol, he took it from her. "Ready to try it loaded?"

"Yes," she said tentatively. All her earlier confidence seemed to drain from her. "At least I think so."

He slid a few bullets in the chamber. "You'll do fine. It's a piece of cake." He handed her the gun. "Aim it at that big fir tree."

She lifted up the gun and pointed it in the direction of the tree, her arm bobbing up and down. He knew she'd never get off a clean shot as long as she kept seesawing the pistol. He came up behind her and slipped his right arm along hers.

"Keep it steady," he said quietly as his hand covered hers. He kept his voice calm and smooth, hoping to boost her confidence. He could feel her shaking against him. Applying slight pressure to her arm with his, he forced it to remain still. "We'll do this on the count of three. One . . ."

"Mr. Jackson—"

"Two."

"I'm not sure I'm ready for this—"

"THREE!"

She squeezed the trigger as soon as the word was out of his mouth. Her quick reflex action surprised him, just as the kick back of the gun surprised her. They were both knocked off balance, and she slammed back into his chest, causing him to take a few steps backward.

She didn't say anything for a long moment, but he could hear the heaviness of her breathing. They remained stock still. Peering around her, he looked at her face to see if she was all right. "Miss Faraday?"

"Oh . . . my . . . lands . . ."

"Uh, maybe we shouldn't have tried this—"

"That was *wonderful*," she said.

He frowned in disbelief. "What?"

"I had no idea there was so much . . . power." She turned in his arms. "No idea at all."

There was a wild-eyed look in her eyes, one that sent his pulse racing like a thoroughbred caught up in the chase. They both still held on to the gun and kept it pointed at the ground. But he wasn't thinking about weapons or bullets or strong kick-backs. He was drowning in the excitement he saw on her face. Beneath the prim and proper surface of Melanie Faraday lay something magnetic and untamed. It drew him to her, an attraction so heady it was difficult for him to breathe.

"Can we do it again?" she asked, her full lips curving into a delightful smile.

He smiled in return, her radiance enveloping him in a cloud of warmth. "You bet we can."

Chapter Ten

The next morning, after breakfast, Luke announced it was time to break camp. Melanie and Rodrigo went to the river to wash the dishes and bring back a jug of water for their next leg of the trip. The other boys helped Luke load the wagon, while Flora took care of Rosalita.

As she wiped the last tin dish, Melanie remembered the time she spent with Luke yesterday learning to shoot. She'd been so terrified of the weapon at the beginning, but by the end of the afternoon she was shooting as if she'd been born with a gun in her hand. The idea that she could do something that had always seemed so difficult and dangerous, and do it well, surprised her. It also bolstered her self-confidence, which had taken more than one blow since they'd started on the Santa Fe Trail.

But more important than that, she'd felt a connection with Luke. Taking her first shot had been exhilarating, but it couldn't compare to the sensation that blasted through her when he'd smiled at her. It hadn't been a perfunctory smile either. The emotion had reached his eyes, causing them to glow with warmth. At that moment, being caught up in the radiance of his smile was almost too much to bear. Even now, the memory was bittersweet.

She frowned. She was treading in dangerous waters here. From that point on, her relationship with Luke had changed. She couldn't pin down the reason why, but all through the evening last night, and even several times this morning, they had exchanged several furtive glances and secret smiles. Clearly a connection had formed between them, one that she truly didn't want to sever. She simply longed to be free to enjoy it. But she couldn't do that.

She debated whether to tell him about Ethan. It would be the right thing to do. She'd started off this trip with a deception, and it was unfair of her to continue to keep secrets from him.

But doubts assailed her. What if she was reading too much into this? Maybe she saw something in Luke's eyes that wasn't really there. If that was true, then bringing up Ethan would be pointless. Besides, she didn't want to think about her betrothed, much less discuss him with Luke.

A sigh escaped her. It was best not to get into it.

"*Senorita?* I have filled the jug."

"*Bueno,* Rodrigo." She rose from the edge of the bank and gathered up the breakfast dishes. "Let's go back to camp."

When they returned, Luke was hitching up the oxen. She tried to avoid watching him, but it was hopeless. The muscles in his broad back and arms rippled beneath his blue army shirt as he hooked up the team to the wagon. His limp was slightly more pronounced than usual, but she now knew that was from morning stiffness. She thought about how much pain the wound must have caused him, and she felt a pinch in her heart.

As if he sensed her looking at him, he turned around. Their eyes met, and a pleasant tingle flew right through her. He smiled.

"Nice day," he said as she approached.

"Yes it is." She glanced down at the dishes in her arms, shyness suddenly overcoming her.

He leaned against the side of one of the oxen. "I have to admit, as beautiful as San Antonio is, nothing beats a Santa Fe sunrise."

Her gaze flew to his. She'd been thinking the exact same thing that morning, when she'd watched the glow of the sun break out while she was fixing breakfast. The soft pastel hues splashed across the sky, tinting the clouds with colors. Enjoying the splendor in the open field, with the majestic mountains as a backdrop, gave her a sense of peace and wonder at God's creation. She was intrigued that he felt the same way.

"We should be hitting the trail soon," he said.

"Will you have any problems getting the wagon out?"

He shook his head. "The ground seems dry enough. This is a strong team. I'm sure they'll manage without a problem." They stared at each other for a moment, his smile widening. "I believe it's going to be a good day."

She basked in his good humor, feeling that unnamed connection once again. She smiled in return. "I think so too."

The oxen pulled the wagon out of the crusty mud without a problem. They started for the trail by mid-morning. Melanie stayed in the back with the children, playing with Rosalita and telling more childhood stories to the boys, even though she kept thinking about sitting next to Luke on the buckboard seat. She'd run out of the fairy tales her mother used to tell her, so she started making up her own. The boys seemed more fascinated with her invented stories than the ones that had been passed down for centuries.

Eventually they did tire of the tales, just as her

imagination ran dry. Soon they all lay down, including Rosalita and Flora. It wasn't long before the others were asleep. But sleep was the furthest thing from Melanie's mind.

She crept out of the wagon and slid into the space next to Luke, welcoming the fresh spring air that filled her senses. He gave her a quick nod, as if he'd expected her to be there, then kept his attention on the trail ahead. She noticed this stretch of dirt road wasn't as bumpy as the one between Santa Fe and Pecos.

"Where are we going?" she asked.

"San Miguel," he replied. "It's very close to the river, so let's hope we don't have another flood."

She gripped the edge of her seat at the thought. "Surely we can't be flooded out twice."

"It could happen." He glanced at her, his lips tilted in a half-grin. "But it's highly unlikely."

"Thank goodness."

He slapped the reins gently against the oxen's flanks. "I thought we might stop in a bit, have something to eat. Let the boys stretch their legs."

She looked at him, more than a little surprised. "Won't that take too much time?"

He shrugged. "Not really. We'll still make San Miguel in plenty of time to set up camp this evening." He glanced at her. "Unless you want to get there sooner."

She wasn't in any hurry to get to Las Vegas, not

anymore. "I think a break would be good. For the boys," she quickly added.

"Right." He cast a sidelong glance. "For the boys."

It turned out the rest stop was beneficial to them all. They all ate lunch, and the children played. Flora laid a blanket down on the soft grass and she and Rosalita basked in the sunlight. Luke sat beneath a small tree, his back and head leaning against the trunk while Melanie cleaned up the dishes.

She made quick work of the task. Wiping her hands on her apron, she looked at him. His legs were drawn up and his forearms rested on each knee. His eyes were closed, and she assumed he was asleep.

Inhaling the fresh air, she turned and watched the boys as they chased each other. Hearing Rosalita giggle, Melanie turned to see Flora tickling the baby's stomach. Melanie smiled, contentment filling her. She hadn't felt such a sense of peace in a long time. Being here with the children, Flora and Luke felt so . . . *right*. She wished she could freeze this moment in time, wanting to forever remember the soft breeze blowing on her back, the outline of the mountains against the blue sky. A single word came instantly to mind. *Happiness*.

She bent down and picked one of the wildflowers dotting the grass at her feet. She examined the unfamiliar lavender bud. "I wonder what this is called?" she wondered out loud.

"I'm not real knowledgeable about flowers."

She jumped.

"I'm sorry. I didn't mean to startle you."

Spinning around, she looked up at him. "That's alright. I didn't even hear you come up behind me."

"I move quietly."

That was one revelation that didn't surprise her. "I guess you learned to in the Army."

"Nope." He grinned. "I learned by sneaking up on stray sheep. You have to be real careful around them. They spook easily."

She chuckled. "I wouldn't know. I've never seen a sheep before."

"Really? You mean sheep don't run up and down the streets of Boston?"

"Oh, sure, right along with the pigs, chickens, and goats." She chuckled, and he smiled. It reached his eyes, causing little crinkles to form at the corners. She remembered when she'd first met him, how his countenance seemed set in stone. Now she sensed it was crumbling slightly, and it delighted her.

She twirled the thin, green stem of the flower between her index finger and thumb, and glanced down at it. "It's quite pretty," she commented.

"So are you."

His words stilled her fingers, and she thought she heard him mumble something under his breath.

"I'm sorry," he said, looking contrite. He glanced down at the ground, then to the side. "I shouldn't have said that."

"Oh," she replied, not sure whether she should be insulted or not.

"Wait, that's not what I meant. I don't know what made me say that . . . well, I do know, but I don't know why I said it out loud."

She knitted her brows together, confused. "What are you talking about?"

He inhaled deeply. "Don't get me wrong. You *are* pretty. I just shouldn't have told you, that's all."

"Well, why on earth not? It's not like a girl doesn't want to hear that's she's pretty."

He tilted up his head and closed his eyes, obviously frustrated. And flustered.

She found his discomfort rather fascinating. Was she having that effect on him?

He looked at her. "Miss Faraday, I've really messed this up. I apologize for being so forward. I don't want you to feel that you're in any kind of danger with me around."

"Danger?"

His skin above his beard turned light pink. "I would never take advantage of you, no matter what. I just want you to know that."

Her own complexion flushed when she caught the meaning of his words. "Mr. Jackson, I can assure you that I feel perfectly safe with you. I know you wouldn't do anything to compromise me or hurt the children."

He looked visibly relieved. "Good. I'm glad we've come to an understanding then." He shoved his hand deep into the pocket of his trousers. The moment between them grew awkward.

"Do you really think I'm pretty?" she blurted out suddenly.

Now it was her turn for regrets. She wanted to bite back the words as soon as they left her mouth. She sounded petulant and childish, like a desperate woman fishing for compliments. But she couldn't help it. She had to know.

He looked at her for a long time. "Yes," he said softly. "I do."

Her breath caught in her throat. It was obvious she hadn't merely fantasized that he felt something for her. Time seemed to melt into slow motion as he brought his hand up to her face and caressed her cheek.

"You're very pretty," he said on a husky whisper.

She could feel the calluses on his palm and the roughness of his fingertips against her skin. His hand was strong, yet gentle, and she had no doubt she would always be safe with this man, under any circumstances. She closed her eyes and leaned into his touch, all the while knowing that she had to put a stop to it right here and now.

With a huge effort, she pulled away and stepped

back from him. It felt like her heart was ripping in two as she did. She couldn't trust herself to speak. Tears stung behind her eyes. Why was life so unfair? Here was a man she was starting to care for, despite everything. Yet she was promised to another.

"Oh, Luke," she said, the formalities between them turning into dust. "I've bungled this badly."

His expression turned to rock. "You've what?"

A knot tightened in her stomach. "There's something . . . something I have to tell you. I—"

A sudden shriek pierced the air, cutting off her words. They both turned to see one of the boys fall to the ground.

"Oh, dear Lord," she cried, picking up her skirt and breaking into a run. "It's Raul."

Luke followed behind and quickly passed her, reaching Raul first. Both Ramon and Rodrigo were kneeling beside their brother, speaking in frantic Spanish. Their words were coming out so fast Melanie had no idea what they were saying.

Fortunately Luke did. "Scorpion," he said, reaching for the boy.

Raul's fierce cries grew louder.

"It stung him right . . . here." He pointed to a red patch on the heel of Raul's hand.

"What should we do?" Melanie asked, feeling at a complete loss. By this time Flora had joined them, holding Rosalita in the sling.

Flora and Luke conversed in Spanish with each

other briefly. She nodded, then handed Rosalita to Melanie and hurried to the wagon. Raul continued to sob and Melanie longed to comfort him. Not only was language a barrier, but she had no idea how to treat a scorpion sting. She hated feeling so helpless.

Flora returned with a wet compress and handed it to Luke. He applied it to the sting. Raul shrieked again and Luke gathered him in his lap. He spoke Spanish in low, comforting tones until Raul's sobs had diminished into sniffles. Luke removed the compress to check the wound. The other two boys crowded around to also have a look at it.

"Is he going to be alright?" Melanie asked, staring at Raul's swollen flesh. From his cries and his skin's reaction to the sting, she knew he had to be in great pain.

Luke nodded, but the somber set of his jaw told Melanie that he was being encouraging for the boy's benefit. Flora crossed herself and said a silent prayer.

Melanie felt the icy fingers of fear grip her heart.

Chapter Eleven

"Y ou can not keep blaming yourself, *senorita.*"
Flora laid Rosalita into her makeshift crib. "It is not
your fault the scorpion stung Raul."

"Yes, it is," Melanie said. She was sitting beside
him as he lay on a blanket in the back of the wagon.
She feathered her fingertips through his damp
bangs. The air was thick and hot, but she barely noticed.

He had finally fallen asleep a few minutes ago.
She clenched her teeth at each jostle and bump the
wheels rolled over. "If I hadn't brought them out
here, if I'd taken the time to think about what I was
doing—"

"If, if, if," Flora said, then clucked her tongue.
"Life is full of ifs. It is pointless to spend all this

time doubting yourself. There are scorpions in Santa Fe too. He could have been stung there."

"I suppose," Melanie said, looking at Raul's small, bandaged hand. His cries of pain still echoed in her ears. Although he was quiet now, his condition was still uncertain.

"We'll have to wait and see," Luke had told her a couple of hours earlier when the two of them were alone.

"Surely we can do more than that," she'd replied, her feelings of powerlessness intensifying. "Maybe Flora has some medicine or some herbs—"

He placed his hand on her arm, silencing her. "There's no treatment for this. We just have to pray that there wasn't a lot of poison in the sting."

So she had prayed. And to her relief since they'd started back on the trail three hours ago Raul hadn't seemed any worse.

He hadn't gotten any better, either.

In the corner of the wagon Ramon and Rodrigo talked with each other, their conversation subdued. It was hard to believe they had been rollicking in the desert grass just hours earlier. The mood among everyone was somber.

"You should lie down and rest, *senorita*," Flora said. "There is nothing you can do for him now."

Melanie shook her head and grasped Raul's healthy hand. "I can comfort him," she whispered, stroking his dirt-stained fingers. "It's the least I can do."

Luke took off his hat and wiped the sweat and trail dust from his forehead. The afternoon had turned hot and oppressive. If he was this uncomfortable outside the wagon, he could only imagine how Melanie and the children felt inside.

Worry dragged at him. Raul's sting looked bad, but he'd seen worse. Trouble was he'd never seen a child that small stung before. Melanie had looked ready to jump out of her skin when he told her that all they could do was wait out the next few hours and watch how the boy reacted. More than anything he wished he could have done something to help him, to ease his pain and take the sting away. Not only for the child's sake, but for Melanie's as well.

He clenched his jaw. Confound it, he was coming to care for these people, something he hadn't expected and had hoped to avoid. The last thing he needed or wanted were complications or entanglements. On this trip he'd gotten both.

Melanie's face appeared in his mind, the lovely blue of her eyes that had sparkled so beautifully when he told her she was pretty. At first he'd wanted to sink into the ground and disappear when he'd said those words. But he'd say them again, over and over, if only to see the look of delight on her face one more time.

But it wasn't just her beauty that touched his heart. Her intense reaction to Raul's sting only confirmed what he'd suspected all along—she loved these children. It made him wonder how she was going to handle it if Raul didn't improve. He didn't really have to wonder, he already knew. "It would devastate her," he whispered out loud. "Her heart would shatter into a thousand pieces."

He reckoned his own heart would break too.

They made camp near San Miguel early in the evening. They camped close to another stretch of the Pecos River and replenished their water supply, filling up two extra jugs. They wouldn't see another river until Las Vegas.

Melanie never left Raul's side, leaving Flora and Luke to cook dinner and ready the other children for bed. However, Rosalita was wide awake. Flora handed her to Luke while she settled Ramon and Rodrigo in the wagon, and checked on Raul.

Luke felt more comfortable holding the baby this time. He patted her on the rump. He tweaked her nose, making her coo. He touched a tuft of her black hair, marveling at its softness. He smiled at her tiny, round face.

"You are very good with her," Flora said, coming up behind him.

"She's a good baby," he replied in Spanish. "At

least, I think so. I don't have any experience with them."

She reached for the coffee pot and poured a cup, setting it on the ground beside him.

"Gracias," he said.

She held out her arms and he placed Rosalita in them. "She's very good," Flora said. "Which is fortunate for us. We've had our share of problems on this trip."

He picked up his cup. "How is Raul?"

"The same. But I think he will recover just fine."

"Good." Hiding the swell of relief that rose within him, he took a sip.

"Don't worry about *Senorita* Faraday," Flora added. "She will be fine too."

"I didn't say I was worried."

"You didn't have to."

He kept quiet and continued to drink his coffee. The sky was clear and the stars were twinkling, like dozens of pinpricks of light against a velvety background. He stared at them, suddenly remembering what Melanie had said right before Raul was stung. Something about bungling badly and that she had something to tell him. In his concern over Raul he'd forgotten about it until that moment. Now it started to nag at him.

He glanced at Flora, who was rocking Rosalita in her arms. He was tempted to ask her about it. Certainly she would know what Melanie was talking about. But he held his tongue. He was positive Flora would never betray Melanie's confidence. He also wanted to hear it straight from Melanie's mouth.

"I believe she's asleep now," Flora said. Carefully she stood up. "I'll go put her to bed. Good night, *Senor* Jackson."

"Buenos noches."

Luke wasn't sure how long he stayed up after Flora left, but by the time he picked up his things the fire was low and the coffee was gone. He headed for the wagon to lay his bedroll underneath it when he heard movement inside. He looked up to see Melanie stepping out through the canvas flaps. Immediately he dropped his belongings and went to help her down.

"Thank you," she said as soon as her feet touched the ground.

He nodded. In the darkness he could barely make out her features, but from the slight slumping of her posture he could tell she was exhausted. "You should get some sleep," he said.

"I will. I needed a drink of water, that's all." She walked over by the campfire and picked up the jug of water, struggling with its heavy weight. He followed her.

"Here, let me." He picked up a cup and filled it, then handed it to her. "Flora says Raul will be alright."

Melanie accepted the cup gratefully. "Thank goodness." She took a long swallow. "I couldn't live with myself if . . . if . . ."

"I know." He touched her shoulder. "But you don't have to dwell on that now."

She nodded and handed him the cup. "Thanks for the drink."

"You're welcome."

"I think I'll go to bed now." She sighed. "I'm so tired."

"I'll help you get in the wagon."

She shook her head. "I can manage. Good night."

He turned and watched her walk away. "Good night," he repeated, disappointed to see her go. He wanted to talk to her, but now wasn't the time. He didn't want to ply her with questions, not when she looked ready to drop at any second. He could wait. They had tomorrow, and the next day . . .

A sharp pain dug at his chest. Tomorrow they would reach Tecolote. Then after that was Las Vegas. They had two more days together, three at the most. Then she would take the children to the Westbrooke's and return to Santa Fe, while he made his way back to San Antonio. He would be free from the Army, free from his responsibilities, and on his way home. The thought should have made him happy. Two days ago it would have made him deliriously so.

Except now he felt anything but happy.

Chapter Twelve

"So how far is Tecolote from here?" Melanie asked.

"Several hours," Luke replied. "We should make it there by tonight."

They were sitting next to each other on the buckboard seat, heading down a well-worn portion of the Santa Fe Trail. Earlier Melanie had continued to stay with Raul in the back of the wagon while the rest of them had broken camp at midday. Finally after a few hours she had emerged, telling Luke that Raul seemed to be on the mend.

"He was asking for a tortilla," she'd said with a weary smile. "I had to give him a biscuit instead."

Luke was relieved to hear the news. "At least now

we know he's alright. Can't keep a growing boy's appetite down for long."

"That's true. I can't believe how much the boys eat! I'm glad we bought so many supplies before we left. As it is we'll barely have enough to make it to Las Vegas." She stared to the side at the passing landscape. "When will we get there?"

"Two days. Three, barring any more disasters."

"Surely we've had more than our share on this trip."

"Amen to that."

Melanie adjusted the tie on her bonnet, and he forced himself not to stare at her. There was something they had to get out in the open between them. Now was as good a time as any to ask her about it.

"Melanie," he started, tightening his grip on the reins. "Before Raul was stung you were trying to tell me something." He paused, attempting to gauge her reaction.

She remained impassive, which puzzled him. Usually her expressions were like an open book.

"I think I should know what it is," he said.

She looked away and he glanced at her. His gaze was drawn to her lap where her hands were tightly clasped together. Her knuckles were stark white. Evidently she was struggling with something important.

He prodded her along. "Whatever it is, you can tell me. I promise not to get angry."

She sighed. "Don't make a promise you can't keep."

"I always keep my promises."

"I know," she said solemnly. "I admire you a lot for that. Among other things," she added softly.

It wasn't so much what she'd said than how she said it that made him smile. "You admire me? That's . . . nice."

"Don't tease," she said petulantly.

"I'm not teasing. I like to be admired." He puffed out his chest in an exaggerated motion. "Does a man's ego good."

Her laugh was genuine this time and he was glad to hear it. Her disposition lightened considerably. "I always suspected you had an amusing side to you."

"Is that so?"

"Yes. You were so stern and cold and gruff when I first met you." She averted her gaze again, as if she regretted voicing her thoughts aloud.

"I'll admit in the beginning I was kind of caught off guard by . . . well, by everything. But now things are different."

She looked back at him. "Why?"

He shrugged. "This trip hasn't been as bad as I expected it to be."

"What?" Her mouth dropped open. "You can't be serious. Flora was sick, we were flooded, I got lost, and now Raul's been stung. That's quite bad in my opinion."

"Yes, but we've made it through just fine."

"And what about all of us? From the very beginning you disliked the children, and you could hardly stand to be around me."

"I didn't know you. And I'll allow I let first impressions—and my own prejudice—sway me. But," he said, turning to her, "I've gotten to know the children now, and they're good kids." He lowered his voice. "I know you better too. I like what I see . . . what I've learned about you. I like it a lot."

She licked her lips. Her lower chin began to tremble slightly and a thin film of moisture appeared in her eyes. "Oh, Luke. You're going to hate me for this."

He frowned deeply. "How could I hate you?" He pulled the wagon to a stop and rotated in his seat so he could face her square on.

"Don't," she whispered. "Don't say anything else." Slowly one tear, then two, then several slid out of the corners of her eyes and rolled down her cheeks. "Oh Luke, I never intended for this to happen."

"I shouldn't have said anything." He slapped the oxen's flanks with the reins. From their grunts he realized he'd hit them harder than he should have. They forged on ahead anyway.

The silence lay thick between them. Now would be a good time for her to chatter, he thought morosely. But she remained quiet. He wasn't about to say anything. He was done talking. Why had he brought it up in the first place? It was unlike him not to think before he spoke. Why did he choose this time to go against his nature?

"Luke, please try to understand," she finally said. "It's complicated."

"Oh, I understand." He set his jaw. "Let's forget the whole thing."

"Luke." She placed her hand on his leg.

He nearly fell out of his seat. The gesture was bold, intimate. He looked at her in surprise. "Melanie?"

Then out of nowhere a ripping pain suddenly shot through his leg. He gasped and stared down at the dark stain seeping through his trousers. An arrow was buried in the middle of his thigh, sticking straight out of his leg.

He whirled a look over his shoulder just in time to feel the whizzing of air against his cheek as another arrow flew by. Horror seized him as he spun back to see if Melanie had been struck. "Thank God you're alright," he exclaimed.

At that point the pain took hold of him. Black dots formed in his vision. He'd been struck near the spot of his war injury. Pain pulsed through his thigh and hip. He heard the sound of approaching hoof beats. With a great effort he looked over his shoulder again to see two men on horseback gaining on them.

"Indians!" Melanie shrieked.

He faced her. Her skin had gone whiter than he'd

ever seen her before. "My gun . . . you have to shoot them."

"Shoot them?" Her voice raised two notches to borderline hysteria. "No, no, I can't do that, I simply can't!" Then she looked at his leg. "You're hurt! Stop the wagon, we have to stop."

He ground his teeth. "We can't stop! They'll overcome us if we do."

"Can't we outrun them?"

"With oxen? Listen to me," he said, swaying in the seat. "I'm dizzy, or I'd do it myself. Pull my gun out of the holster and aim it over my shoulder. Try to get off a clean shot."

His vision blurred, and he thought he might pass out. From her hesitation he also thought she would protest again. But instead she reached for his holster, flipped up the cover, and unsheathed his gun. He leaned forward to give her a clear target. She gripped the barrel with both hands.

"One," he heard her say. "Two. THREE!"

The gun fired and she fell back, tottering on the seat. The noise had startled the oxen, and they veered off the trail. Luke held onto the reins as tightly as he could and pulled them back. The effort sent shards of pain crashing through him.

Then everything went black.

Chapter Thirteen

"Luke? Luke? Can you hear me?"

Luke worked to open his eyes. Through narrowed slits he saw Melanie hovering over him. He barely sensed her hand against his forehead.

"Please, please wake up," she pleaded.

"Melanie?" he managed to croak.

"Oh, thank God!"

He felt a drop of wetness strike his cheek and he knew she was crying. "Don't," he whispered.

"I'm sorry . . . I can't help it."

He opened his eyes wider now. His vision fixed on the outline of sparse treetops behind her, and he sensed he was lying on the ground. "Where are we?"

"I really don't know. You passed out, and I had to take the reins."

"You steered the team?"

She nodded. "After I realized the Indians weren't after us anymore. I pulled the wagon off the trail and Ramon helped me get you down. You started to stir as soon as we set you on the ground."

He tried to absorb what she'd said. Things were becoming more coherent, and that included the pain. He felt the arrow still sticking in his leg. "Are you sure they're gone?"

"The Indians?"

He nodded.

"Yes. I shot one of them in the arm. He fell from his horse, and the other one turned around and went to him. When the injured one got back in the saddle they took off in another direction."

Relief shook through him. "Nice shot," he said, giving her a small smile, although it was difficult through the pain.

She took his hand. "Thanks."

His smile faded. "Where are the boys?"

"Over by the wagon. I told them not to go far."

"Good. We don't know how many more Indians are around here." He looked at her intently. "We may have to stay here tonight."

"Do you think they'll come back?" she asked, obviously worried.

"I doubt it. There were only two of them, right?"

"Yes."

"Probably drifters, rogues that broke away from

their tribe. If you wounded one of them, they'll stay away. We'll be fine here."

"Good. You're in no condition to travel anywhere."

"Well, we'll see about that. Once I get the arrow out I'll be as good as new." He tried to smile again, but the agonizing ache in his leg wouldn't allow him. "Can you sit me up?"

She helped him lean back against the closest tree. He looked down at his leg and his stomach rolled. He flashed back to his last battle in the war, when the Mexican's bullet had pierced his thigh. The arrow had landed mere inches from that same spot. The blood on his trousers had stopped spreading. He knew it would start up again once he yanked out the arrow.

No time like the present.

Steeling himself, his hand gripped the arrow's shaft.

Melanie drew in her breath. "What are you doing?"

"What does it look like?" he said through gritted teeth. "This thing has to come out."

"But you can't—you shouldn't be doing this—"

He tugged, and the first burst of pain exploded in his leg. His hand started to shake, but he didn't let go. "One . . . more . . . time . . ."

Her hand folded over his. "Stop."

He looked at her, affected by the empathy he saw

in her eyes. She shared his pain too. "It has to come out, Melanie."

"I know." She extracted his hand from the arrow. "Let me do it."

Melanie's stomach twisted and rolled as she looked at the arrow sticking out of Luke's leg. She held the shaft in her hand, and prayed for the strength she needed to pull it out. She looked at the wagon and saw the boys standing there. "Ramon!" she called out.

"Si, senorita?"

"Bring me some clean rags and a water jug. And ask Flora for her small bottle of whiskey."

"Whiskey?" Luke asked.

"For medicinal purposes," Melanie replied, turning to him. His skin was ghostly white beneath his silky beard, and his eyes were filled with pain. He had to be in agony, yet he'd only cried out once, when the arrow had hit his bad leg. After that everything had been a blur to her, from the moment she shot the Indian until the time Ramon had helped her drag Luke, unconscious, from the buckboard seat.

But now everything was crystal clear, and she wished it wasn't. She hated seeing the anguish on his face, the blood staining his pants leg. She didn't want to pull out this arrow. She was loath to cause him more pain than he was already in.

Yet she had no other choice.

"Are you sure about this?" Luke asked, as if he'd read her thoughts.

She swallowed and tried not to glance at his leg. Taking his hand again, she said, "I'm sure. I'll try not to hurt you."

"Don't worry about that. I can handle it. Just get it out." He fumbled with his pocket and pulled out a pocketknife. "Here," he said, handing it to her. "You'll have to cut my trousers."

Nodding, she accepted the knife and cut a wide slit around the wound. The arrow was embedded deep into his flesh. A fresh wave of nausea assaulted her.

Ramon sprinted toward them, carrying the cloths and the bottle. Rodrigo lagged behind, staggering a bit as he hauled the big water jug. He placed it on the ground beside her.

"Gracias, chicos," she said. "Now, go back to the wagon and make sure Raul is okay."

"We can not stay and watch?" Ramon asked.

She looked up at them, incredulous. *She* didn't even want to stay and watch. "Absolutely not," she hissed. "I'm anxious enough as it is without you two hovering over me. Now *go.*"

"All right, we are going." Reluctantly they left, dragging out their steps as they went to the wagon.

"Imagine that," she mumbled, picking up the

whiskey bottle. "Wanting to watch something like this."

"They're boys," Luke said dimly. "I'd be more concerned if they *didn't* want to watch."

"How can you joke at a time like this?"

"Who's joking?"

She opened the bottle of whiskey. "I'm going to pour this on the wound," she told him.

He sucked his breath through his teeth when the alcohol hit his leg. "Let me have that," he rasped, taking the bottle from her. He took a swig. "For medicinal purposes."

She gripped the arrow, forcing her nausea down. "Ready?"

"Just yank the blasted thing already!" he snapped.

Knowing it was the pain talking, she didn't take offense. With a great effort she pulled as hard and straight as she could, feeling the arrow tear through muscle and flesh as she did. The sensation sickened her.

He didn't cry out, but took another long drink of the whiskey.

Quickly she placed a folded cloth on the wound, and applied pressure to staunch the blood.

"How did you know to do that?" Luke asked, his eyes closed. He gripped the whiskey bottle tightly in his hand. "Take care of wounds, I mean?"

"My mother taught me, before she died. She was very curious about medicine and healing, and had read lots of books on the subject. She took care of all our illnesses and wounds, as well as the servants." She lifted the pad, saw the blood still seeping, and pressed down on it again. "I just wish she could have healed herself," she said, unable to keep the note of sadness out of her voice.

He didn't say anything. She cast a look at him and saw that his eyes were still closed. She assumed he'd passed out again, but he opened one eye, then closed it again. "Thanks," he said, his voice barely audible. "I'm feeling better now."

She doubted that, but kept her thoughts to herself. He wasn't out of danger yet. If infection set in, he could lose his life. But that was too horrible to contemplate, so she shoved the thought completely away, forcing herself to concentrate on bandaging the hole in his thigh.

Lifting up the cloth pad again, she saw the bleeding had stopped. She also saw the ugly scar that was a little larger than a bullet right next to the arrow wound.

When she'd tied the last strip of cloth around his leg, she touched his shoulder. "Luke?" she said tentatively.

He opened his eyes. "I'm still here."

"Will you be alright for a couple of minutes? I need to ask Flora something."

"I'll be fine," he said, closing his eyes again.

"I'll be right back." She stood up and hurried to the wagon. Flora was holding Rosalita in the sling. Raul still looked pale and tired from his ordeal with the scorpion, but he was sitting down on the ground eating another biscuit. Ramon and Rodrigo were drawing pictures in the dirt with sticks.

"Flora, did you bring your medicine kit?"

"*Si*, it is in the back, near Rosalita's crib beneath the blankets."

"Do you have anything in it that will work on fever? In case Mr. Jackson gets an infection?"

"I think so. I will check. How is he doing?"

Melanie looked at him for a moment. "Amazingly well. Under the circumstances."

"He is a strong *hombre*. He will be fine, I am sure of it."

Melanie felt a tug on her skirt. She glanced down, and saw Raul staring up at her. He said something in Spanish, and although she knew he was asking a question she wasn't sure what it was. "Flora?" she queried her chaperone.

"He wants to know if *Senor* Jackson will be alright. Our little Raul is very worried about him."

Kneeling down beside the boy, she looked into his face. "He will be fine," she said. *"Bueno."*

His expression betrayed his relief. He leaned against her, and slowly she wrapped her arms around him, drawing him to her. Her eyes closed when he returned her embrace.

He stepped away from her and smiled, and then went to join his brothers. She let out a deep breath.

"He is full of surprises, that one," Flora said. "You go back to *Senor* Jackson, and I will check my supplies—he needs you now."

"*Gracias,* Flora. Thank you for everything. You've been a lifesaver to me on this trip."

"I could not let your father down. Or you." She tilted her head in Luke's direction. "Now, go see to him."

Melanie spun around and returned to Luke. He appeared to be resting comfortably, in spite of everything. She lowered herself beside him and examined his leg from a distance. A bit of blood had soaked through the bandage, but it was holding.

She dropped her face in her hands and started to shake. Exhaustion consumed her and her emotions were in a whirlwind. So much had happened in the past few days she could scarcely comprehend it all. A natural disaster, a scorpion sting, now an attack by two rogue Indians—and they were little more than halfway to Las Vegas. What else could happen to them on this trip?

"I was right, wasn't I?"

Startled by his voice, she looked at him. His eyes were hooded and barely open. "Right about what?"

"The trail is a dangerous place."

Guilt came upon her in crashing waves. "I'm so sorry."

"There you go, apologizing again. You don't have to."

"Yes I do. This was a horrible idea, simply horrible. I've put people I care about in danger. I've involved them into this ill-conceived plan of mine. And who gets hurt? Flora. Raul. You." She paused. "I wish it had been me."

His eyes flew wide open. "Don't ever say something so foolish again."

"Why shouldn't I? I deserve to be lying there, not you." She looked away. "You must hate me."

He grasped her hand, his grip surprisingly strong. "Enough with the martyr stuff, okay? It gets tiring after a while."

"Pardon me?"

"Blaming yourself, wishing yourself harm, how is that going to help? Things happen, and I believe they happen for a reason."

"How reasonable is it for you to get shot in the leg? Or for Raul to get stung?"

"I don't know. And at this point I don't care. It happened, now I have to heal. That's what I'm focusing on, not casting blame." He ran his thumb across the back of her hand and looked at it. "You're covered in blood," he murmured. "My blood. You should . . . you should wash it off."

"I will." But she didn't move, mesmerized by the glide of his thumb over her skin, amazed by his absolution of her guilt.

"I don't hate you," he said quietly.

Her fragile emotions came close to crumbling at the kindness in his voice. Suddenly Ethan, her betrothed, and even her father didn't matter. Only Luke did.

He was strong and unyielding on the outside, but with a gentle and kind soul. He was loyal and trustworthy to the core. He could make her seethe with frustration one minute and have her laughing the next. He had so many facets. She liked discovering each one, and wanted to find out more.

His eyes were closed again, and he was resting.

Moving closer to him, she grasped his hand in both of hers. Then in her boldest move yet, she leaned forward and kissed him softly on the mouth, lingering there for a few long moments. When she felt him respond, she quickly drew apart from him.

Then she ran away.

Chapter Fourteen

When Melanie kissed him, Luke knew he had just experienced a slice of heaven. The pain in his leg had seemed to disappear when she'd pressed her mouth to his. And although she had caught him totally by surprise, he wouldn't have minded if the kiss lasted forever.

But then, inexplicably, she ran off.

The woman baffled him in every way. When he tried to express his feelings for her, she cut him off. Then a short time later she ended up kissing him. It was enough to make a sane man lose his mind completely.

Instead, he was losing his heart.

He leaned his head back against the tree. Pain throbbed through his leg. His mind let go of

Melanie for the moment as he analyzed their situation. He couldn't stand up. Tomorrow might be different, he might be able to hop into the wagon, but he couldn't drive the team, not as weak as he was.

He also thought about the Indians. He'd assured Melanie they weren't coming back, but that had been more to keep her calm than anything else. Truth was they and any number of Indians could attack them at any time, and overcome them easily.

Great protection he was. Right now he doubted he could hold a gun steady.

Looking up, he saw Raul walking toward him. When he reached the tree the boy sat down next to him, but didn't say anything. He curled his knees up to his chest and rested his chin on them.

Luke found comfort in the child's silent company. Tentatively he touched Raul's dark hair. When the boy didn't pull away, he skimmed his palm across it, and then touched his bony shoulder. "*Gracias*," he whispered.

Raul's nod was barely perceptible, but he scooted closer to Luke.

Melanie fled to the wagon and ducked inside. Her breath came in short spurts as she realized what she'd done. She'd kissed Luke Jackson! Of all the reckless things she'd done on this trip, that one topped them all. She shook her head, not knowing whether to laugh or cry. The kiss had been impossibly sweet, his lips impossibly soft. It made her long to kiss him again. But she couldn't. She should have never done it in the first place. *What must he think of me?*

"Senorita?"

Melanie froze at the sound of Flora's voice. She hadn't known anyone was in the wagon. Slowly she turned and saw Flora place Rosalita in her crib. Their gazes met, and Flora's eyebrows shot upward. Melanie flushed and turned away.

"What happened?" Flora asked.

Melanie struggled to compose herself. She began shuffling through the clothing and blankets as if searching for something important. "I don't know what you're talking about."

"Yes, you do, *senorita.*"

Melanie faced her, stunned by the knowing look in Flora's eyes.

"You look different to me somehow," Flora said, tilting her head and studying Melanie's face. Then she sucked in a breath. "You are liking *Senor* Jackson!"

Melanie turned away. "Certainly not!" she insisted. "You've gone *loco*, Flora."

Flora set Rosalita in her crib and moved hurriedly to Melanie. "I have three daughters, *chica.* I have seen that look on their faces before. Pain and joy mixed together." She grasped Melanie's hand. "Please tell me you have not fallen in love with *Senor Jackson.*"

"Would that be such a terrible thing?"

"Yes . . . no." Flora squeezed Melanie's hand. "*Senor* Jackson is a good man. I can see how you could like him."

"I don't know how I feel, Flora. I'm so confused."

"Confusion or no, you must put those feelings away! You are betrothed to someone else."

"Someone I don't love, someone I don't even know," Melanie said sourly. "And I haven't been consulted in the matter at all. How can Father expect me to blindly agree to marry a stranger?"

"Then you should have told him how you felt. Before he left for Albuquerque."

"I know." Melanie stared down at her hand clasped in Flora's, noting the contrasting paleness of her skin against the older woman's olive tone. "But I couldn't. I've never gone against his wishes before. There was never a reason to."

Flora remained silent for a moment. "Have you told *Senor* Jackson about *Senor* Vincent?"

Melanie shook her head. "There won't be a *Senor* Vincent, at least not in my life. When we get back to Santa Fe I'll tell Father that I can't marry Ethan."

"Are you planning to marry *Senor* Jackson?"

She sighed heavily, but didn't respond.

Flora touched her fingertips to her temple. "*Dios mio*, this is a mess."

"I've made a big fool of myself." She held up her hand when Flora started to speak. "Don't ask."

"Alright. But *senorita*, why break off the engagement with *Senor* Vincent?"

"Because I will not marry a man I do not love! I simply can't do it."

Flora's lips thinned. "What if your father is against this? What if he insists on you going through with your engagement?"

"He wouldn't do that," Melanie replied. "He's never been unreasonable before." Yet she wasn't completely certain. Hadn't promising her to another man been unreasonable in the extreme? It was almost as if she didn't know her father anymore, that he had changed into someone else the minute they'd stepped foot on Santa Fe soil.

"I hope not." Flora cupped Melanie's cheeks in both of her hands. "For your sake," she said, her tone melting into kindness and filled with sympathy. "And I suspect for *Senor* Jackson's as well."

A short time later Melanie got out of the wagon and looked over at Luke. She watched as Raul inched closer to him. The scene touched her. Somehow those two, at complete odds a few days ago, were now drawing comfort from each other. She never would have thought it possible. Yet so many impossible things had happened on their journey.

She turned away from them and continued to gather up sticks as she and the other two boys and Flora set up camp. She tried to put her kiss with Luke out of her mind as she focused on reality. They would have to stay here for a couple of days while Luke mended, setting back their arrival in Las Vegas even further. As it was they had been on the trail for a week, and they still had lots of miles ahead of them. Luke couldn't be happy about that.

The fact that it was up to her and Flora to take care of everything suddenly penetrated into Melanie's mind. A streak of fear flashed through her. What if the Indians came back? They were practically defenseless, except for her newly achieved skill with Luke's pistol. They couldn't possibly ward off an Indian attack.

Her hands shook as she picked up a twig, and she fought for calm. She had to be strong, for all their sakes. Breaking down into a puddle of tears wouldn't help their situation at all. There was no use fretting over something that hadn't happened yet. If they were attacked, she'd deal with it then.

Her courage bolstered, she took her bundle of kindling and laid it in a pile. The boys had found several large rocks and placed them in a circle. Shortly Melanie would start a fire in the ring, and then she would start dinner. As she continued to make plans, she felt more in control of herself and her emotions.

But that control instantly slipped away when she heard the sound of hoof beats in the distance.

The others heard it too. Ramon's and Rodrigo's kindling spilled to the ground as they stared in the direction of the thundering sound. Melanie barely heard Flora as she came up behind her.

"*Senorita?* Is that—"

"Yes," she said, her voice coming out in a petrified squeak. "They're coming."

Instantly she sprung into action. "Flora, take the boys and help Luke to the wagon. We'll hide behind it."

The three of them left without a word. Melanie dashed inside the wagon and found the pistol. She glanced at Rosalita, who was still asleep, her angelic face filled with peace.

A lump lodged in Melanie's throat. Swallowing past it, she quickly prayed for them all.

She clambered out of the wagon in time to see Luke arrive. Somehow he'd found the strength to hop on one foot with support from Flora and Ramon. Sweat glistened above his brow. He looked at Melanie. "Get my shotgun," he said, breathing heavily.

"But—"

"Just do it!"

She ran to the front of the wagon and grabbed his gun, which was lying on the floorboard of the seat. As fast as she could she dashed back to everyone else. She handed the gun to Luke, but kept the pistol.

"Rosalita!" Flora gasped. "She is inside."

"She'll be safer there," Luke said.

"Yes, Flora," Melanie agreed. "She's still asleep."

The hoof beats grew louder, but they were steady. "They're not in a hurry," Luke said. "They must not know we're here."

Melanie heard a whimper. Raul had started crying. Ramon put his arm around his little brother.

Luke turned and looked at the boys. "I know you're scared, *chicos*. It's okay to be scared. Heck, I'm scared too. But we have to be brave. All of us." His gaze went to Melanie.

She saw the courage in his eyes, and it boosted her own. Gripping the gun, she asked, "What do you want us to do?"

He glanced at Flora. "Keep the boys quiet." Then he looked back at Melanie, his gaze penetrating and intense. "You just be ready to shoot."

He twisted until he was lying on his stomach, his hips turned to the side so most of his weight rested on his good leg. Still, she knew he had to be in intense pain. Yet he didn't utter a sound. Leaning on his elbows, he balanced his weapon and aimed it at the open field straight ahead. Melanie did the same.

Her heart raced and her blood pounded in her ears. She tried not to think about death, but she couldn't help it. All their lives cut short, the children's before they had a chance to truly live theirs. She fought the tears that flooded her eyes, and waited. Waited for the attack.

The riders were just about on top of them when Luke held up his hand. "Hold on," he said, uncocking his rifle. "Those aren't Indians! Hallelujah, they're soldiers."

"Soldiers?" Melanie gasped.

"Yes, praise God." He looked at her, grinning. "We're safe, Melanie. Safe."

She uncocked the pistol and dropped it to the ground, her entire body quaking. Behind her she could hear the boys and Flora speaking rapid-fire Spanish, and although the words meant nothing to her, their joyous tone told her everything. She lowered her head and sobbed with relief.

"It's okay," Luke said, touching her arm and giving it a squeeze. "I told you we're safe."

She nodded, wiping tears from her cheeks. "It's just that—"

"I know," he said softly. "But you were brave, Melanie, and I'm proud of you. You're the strongest, most courageous woman I've ever met."

"You can come out," someone shouted at the edge of their camp. "We're not here to harm you."

"Help me up," Luke said, inching back from the wagon.

Melanie and the boys complied. He wrapped his arm around her shoulders for support and did the same to Ramon. Together they helped him limp around to where a stern soldier sat on a tall horse.

With a weary arm Luke saluted. "We're mighty glad to see you."

The stern faced man scanned him from head to toe, taking in Luke's dirt-caked uniform. He saluted back. "What happened to you, soldier?"

"Indians." Luke explained about their attack. When he finished, his body started to sway. "I think I'll be sitting down now."

To Melanie's surprise, he slid to the ground. As she gently guided him to a lying position, she called out to Flora. "Bring the medicine kit, *pronto!*"

The soldier jumped down from his horse and knelt beside Luke. "Arrow wound?"

"Yes," Melanie said, brushing Luke's sweat-soaked bangs out of his eyes. They were closed, and he had passed out. She glanced at his leg, blanching when she saw blood seeping through the bandage.

The soldier followed her gaze. "Our regiment isn't far behind me," he said. "Luckily we have a surgeon with us. He'll take a look at it." He glanced at her. "Where are you headed?"

"Las Vegas," she said, still focusing on Luke.

"Who else is in your party?"

"My chaperone, Flora, and four children."

He nodded, his gray eyes calm and reassuring. "We're on our way to Fort Bent. We'll escort you to your destination." He jumped to his feet. "I'll ride back and tell them you have wounded. Is anyone else hurt?"

"No."

"Good. I'll return with the rest of the soldiers."

Relief poured through her. Luke would get medical help. They would all be protected. It was almost too good to be true. She tenderly touched Luke's pale cheek, allowing her fingertip to trail down the softness of his beard. "Please, sir. Do hurry."

The soldier tipped his hat. "Don't worry, ma'am. I will."

Chapter Fifteen

"How are you feeling, son?"

Luke looked up at the man standing over him. He could tell from the soldier's uniform that he was a captain, most likely the commanding officer of this regiment. He had a kind, but battle-weary visage. "Better, sir. Thanks for asking."

Luke glanced around and saw that he was lying on a cot beneath a canvas tarp. The last thing he remembered was telling a soldier about the Indian attack. Now he was resting comfortably in a makeshift Army tent.

"Glad to hear it. I hate to see a good soldier die." His expression grew solemn. "You survived the war. It would be a shame if you couldn't survive the victory."

Luke nodded. He couldn't agree more. "We were lucky you came along, sir. I thought we were under attack again."

"No need to worry about that now." The captain rocked back and forth on his heels. "As we told Miss Faraday, we'll escort your group to Las Vegas."

"Where are you headed?"

"Fort Bent."

Luke pondered that for a moment. He was expected to go to Fort Bent after he arrived in Las Vegas. He would get his discharge and then head home.

But how could he do that now? How could he leave Melanie behind to fend for herself? More important, he didn't *want* to leave her behind.

"Mr. Jackson? Are you okay?"

"Yes, sir . . . I'm fine. Just a pang in my leg, that's all." But the pang wasn't in his leg.

It was in his heart.

Night fell across the sky. With the exception of three small campfires, the trail was bathed in darkness. Melanie paced in front of her own fire, rubbing her hands up and down her arms. The boys, exhausted from the day's adventures, were already fast asleep. Flora had retired to tend to Rosalita, and from the lack of sound in the wagon Melanie assumed they were all settled in for the night.

But she couldn't sleep. She was worried about Luke, wondering how he was. Once the soldiers had arrived they whisked him away, treating him as one of their own. Of course he was, even though they weren't in the same regiment. Despite the soldiers' courteous behavior toward her, Flora and the children, Melanie still felt unsettled.

She didn't like being separated from Luke. Not at all.

She continued to pace. She supposed she could go see him. No one would think it odd that she would want to check on his welfare. Yet something held her back. If she was honest with herself, she knew exactly what it was. She was embarrassed. How could she face him after she'd thrown herself at him a few hours ago? It was different when they thought they were under attack. At that point her foolish actions beneath the tree had been temporarily forgotten. Her focus had been solely on survival.

However, they were all safe now, and Luke was getting the medical attention he needed. She couldn't avoid him forever, and she didn't want to. Eventually she'd have to explain herself to him sooner or later.

Perhaps she was making a big deal out of nothing. She should just forget it ever happened. He probably already had.

Except that she couldn't. Every time she closed her eyes she relived that short, sweet kiss. It would be burned in her memory for eternity.

She circled around the fire a few more times, her

emotions completely out of sorts. Finally she couldn't take it anymore. She had to see him, if only to make sure he was truly alright.

She marched over to the tent where Luke had been taken. Several men slept on the ground around the campfire, and she quietly tiptoed around them, not wanting to disturb their slumber. There were several other soldiers keeping night watch on the perimeter of the camp. She surmised they took on the task in shifts.

Winding around the last sleeping figure, she headed for the tent when someone called her name. "Miss Faraday?"

Turning around, she saw the captain of the regiment sitting near the fire, a small lit lantern beside him. A book lay open in his lap. "I'm sorry I bothered you, Captain Davis," she said.

"That's quite all right. I'm just reading my evening devotions."

Melanie glanced at the book and noticed it was a Bible.

"May I be of assistance to you somehow?"

She fidgeted with the waistband of her skirt, suddenly overcome with nervousness. "I-I wanted to see how Mr. Jackson was doing."

"He's doing fine. Resting comfortably last time I checked."

"Thank goodness," she said, breathing more easily now. "I'm glad you're able to take care of him."

She paused for a moment. Luke was well. That's what she wanted to know. There was no reason for her to stay. Despite that, she didn't walk away.

"You can go ahead and see him, if you'd like," the captain said when she didn't leave. "He may be sleeping, but I'm sure he wouldn't mind the company."

"Thank you, sir." There was no turning back now. Melanie pivoted on her heel and stood in front of the tent, her nerves attacking her again. Inhaling a fortifying breath, she forced herself to go inside.

He was sleeping, as the captain had presumed. The light was dim, the only illumination coming from the campfire outside the tent. She watched him from a short distance away, his hands folded across his chest, his breathing slow and steady. She longed to go to him, but her feet refused to move. Instead she resigned herself to gaze at him, thankful once again that he was alright.

Many long moments passed before she made a move to leave. His voice stopped her. "Melanie."

Cautiously she faced him. "I thought you were asleep."

"I was." He turned his head to the side, looking in her direction. "I was dreaming you were here."

A tiny gasp caught in her throat. "You were?"

"Yes. And I'm glad to see it wasn't a dream."

His words, the soft intimate quality of his tone, rendered her speechless for a second. She wished she could see his face, but his features were shadowed. "How are you feeling?"

"Better."

"That's good, I'm glad. That's all I wanted to know, I didn't mean to wake you up, you can go back to sleep now as I'll be leaving."

The sound of his light chuckling filled the tent. "You're babbling, Miss Faraday."

"Sorry."

"Why are you in such a hurry to leave?"

Squinting, she tried to gauge his expression in the darkness of the tent, but she couldn't. "I-I thought you'd want me to go."

"Now why would I want you to do that?" She heard him shift on the cot.

"You must admit it's hardly proper for me to be here without a chaperone," she said, using propriety as an excuse. But it was a weak one, and she knew it. He knew it too.

"I'm laid up on this cot. Nothing inappropriate could possibly happen. Besides, I would never do anything to damage your reputation. I hope you know that."

"I do," she said.

"There's a lantern on the floor near your left. The match sticks are right next to it. Go ahead and light it."

She lit the lamp. A low, yellow glow filled the cramped tent.

"That's better. Now you can see straight into this tent from the outside," Luke said. "Just as good as a chaperone, don't you think?"

She wanted to answer him, but she couldn't. Her mouth had turned dry from the tender expression in his eyes. He'd never looked at her with such endearment before.

"Mr. Jackson—"

"Call me Luke," he said. "We're pretty much past formalities, don't you think?"

"Luke." She loved the sound of his name on her lips.

"May I call you Melanie?"

She nodded, unable to speak.

"Melanie. A very pretty name. I've always thought so."

"Thank you." She blushed, more than a trifle confused. "Mr. Jack—I mean Luke . . . what exactly is going on here?"

He smiled, his teeth gleaming through the thickness of his beard. "What do you mean?"

"You're speaking strangely . . . acting strangely. The medicine they gave you must have been very strong."

"I didn't take any medicine. Didn't need to, the surgeon said it wasn't necessary."

"Oh."

He lifted up his hand and gestured to her. "Can you come a little closer?" When she didn't move right away, he said, "Don't be afraid, I'm not going to bite."

"I'm not afraid . . . of you." But she was afraid. Afraid of the power of her feelings. Afraid that she would spill out the emotions in her heart as easily as milk pouring into a cup. Still, she went to his side, unable to resist his request.

His voice was low. "We need to talk."

"It's about that kiss, isn't it?" she spouted out. She glanced away. She couldn't look at him when she was this embarrassed. "I just want you to know I don't make a habit of going around and kissing men."

"I certainly hope not."

Her gaze met his and she could see the teasing glint in his eyes. "This isn't funny."

He sobered immediately. "No. It's anything but funny."

Where was a thunderstorm when she needed it? Any diversion to interrupt this conversation would be welcome. At least that way she could flee into the night with some dignity intact. However, it was beyond too late to do that. Her dignity had dissolved the moment she'd given in to her impulses and pressed her mouth to his.

"I'm sorry I kissed you," she said. "It won't happen again." Spinning around, she hurried to leave.

"Melanie. Wait."

Something stirred outside the tent. "I really should go," she said, almost desperate to get away from him and the web of kindness he was spinning around her.

"Alright." He looked at her intently. "By the way, I didn't mind the kiss."

Her face heated even more. "You didn't?"

"Not at all." He smiled again. "Good night, Melanie."

"Good night," she said, numbly picking up the lantern and blowing out the light. She set the lantern down and left the tent. Her thoughts were so consumed with what Luke had said she barely missed bumping into the captain.

"Ah, Miss Faraday, I was just getting ready to turn in." He clutched his Bible in his left hand. "How is the patient?"

"Fine," she said, unwilling to elaborate on anymore than that.

"I thought so. He seems like the kind of lad who bounces back quickly. We'll be heading for Tecolote about mid-morning. I'll send two soldiers to help you pack up your things. They'll also drive the wagon."

"That's very kind of you," she said. "We appreciate it."

"You're welcome. Although I relieved Mr. Jackson of his duty this afternoon, I wanted to offer my assurance that you and your party will be well taken care of." He tipped his hat in her direction. "See you in the morning, Miss Faraday," he said, and then walked away.

Melanie stood still. Relieved of duty? He wasn't responsible for her and the children anymore and he had fulfilled his obligation.

With every step back to the wagon her melancholy grew. She hadn't expected it to end like this, hadn't expected it to hurt so much. She'd counted on at least a couple of more days traveling with him. Now they would be traveling separately, and would go their separate ways once they reached Las Vegas.

Her legs felt as heavy as her heart as she climbed in the wagon. She glanced around at the sleeping children, and pain gripped her once more. Soon they would say good-bye.

The boys and Rosalita would be safe and well taken care of by the Westbrookes, she reassured herself for the hundredth time. They would have a future, a brighter one than they would have had on the streets of Santa Fe. She found a tiny amount of consolation in that.

Now she just had to find a way to accept it. Somehow she had to accept leaving both Luke and the children behind. She laid her head down and stretched out the best she could in the crowded wagon. But instead of finding a way to accept her sorrow she found tears. She cried rivers of them before she fell asleep.

Chapter Sixteen

Just as Captain Davis had said, they headed for Te-colote in the morning. The two soldiers he'd sent had packed up Melanie's wagon with crisp efficiency. One was tall and thin with carrot-colored hair. The other one was smaller, with a barrel-like chest and bulky arms that strained the fabric of his faded shirt. They were polite and courteous to all of them, and gentle with the team of oxen.

But the boys eyed them warily. They weren't Luke. Melanie knew that no one would take his place in their hearts, or in her own.

She didn't see a single sign of Luke for the rest of the day. Even when they stopped for lunch and to water and rest the horses and oxen, he stayed with the soldiers. It was out of necessity. But she missed him terribly. If she hated being separated by this short of distance, how could she stand it when hundreds of miles were between them?

They stopped later that evening. The red-headed soldier informed them that they were a few miles past Tecolote as they helped them set up camp.

"We made good time today," he said, whipping off his hat and shaking the dust off it. "We should be in Las Vegas by sunset tomorrow."

"Great," Melanie said flatly.

The children, along with Flora and Melanie, ate their dinner in silence. A few feet away the two soldiers had set up their camp, including a small tent. In the distance she could hear the other men in the regiment talking and laughing. She wondered if Luke was among them, enjoying the camaraderie of his fellow soldiers.

The stocky soldier wiped his mouth with the sleeve of his shirt. "You cook up a fine stew, Miss Faraday. Just like Ma makes back home in Kansas."

"Thank you."

He and the other soldier stood up. "If it's alright with you, we'll be stepping aside for a little while."

"For our evening smoke," the red-haired man chimed in.

"Go right ahead," Melanie said, rising and picking up the dishes. The boys had already finished and Flora was feeding Rosalita. "We'll be fine here."

They nodded and headed over to the rest of the

soldiers. Thick streams of cigarette and pipe smoke wafted above a small group of the men.

Melanie gathered up the rest of their eating utensils and carried them to a bucket of water. She made quick work of washing, drying, and putting them away. By the time she finished and went back to the fire, Flora was sitting there with Rosalita.

"Our journey is almost over," Flora said.

Melanie stared at the crackling fire. "Yes, it is."

Flora kissed Rosalita's cheek. "I have to say, I will miss the children very much. They have worked their way inside my heart."

"Mine too." She looked at Rosalita. "May I hold her?"

"Of course," Flora replied, handing her the baby. "I'll see to the boys. They have been very quiet today. I think they are missing *Senor* Jackson." She gave Melanie a knowing look. "I know they are not the only one."

As Flora walked away, Melanie stared down into Rosalita's face. Her little mouth puckered into a half-smile, bringing tears to Melanie's eyes. "How I will miss you, little one," she said in a broken whisper. "I will miss you all."

"I think these will work for you," the surgeon said, handing Luke a pair of wooden crutches.

Luke examined them as he sat up on the side of the cot, his legs stretched before him on the floor.

He was hurting, but he'd pass out in agony before letting the other man know about it. He was determined to see Melanie, regardless of his discomfort. Shoving one crutch under his armpit he said, "Let's try them out."

"Hold on there," the surgeon piped up. "I said I'd bring you the crutches, but you can't use them until tomorrow."

"Tomorrow? Why not tonight?"

"Because you need to stay off that leg. That arrow caused a lot of damage to an already wrecked part of your thigh. If you want it to heal properly you need to rest. In fact I think tomorrow is too soon, but seeing we'll be in Las Vegas by the end of the day—"

"That quick?"

"Yep. That quick. I'm not so sure why you're in such a hurry to get back on your feet."

"I wanted to check on Miss Faraday and the children."

"But you've been relieved of duty." The surgeon took the crutches and placed them on the far side of the room. "They're not your responsibility anymore. Besides, Rusty and Earl have been taking good care of them."

Luke refused to explain that his wanting to see Melanie had nothing to do with "duty." He stared at the crutches. He'd have to hop on one foot to get to them.

"Don't even think about it," the other man said, visually tracking Luke's line of sight.

Luke cast him an annoyed look, then slumped his shoulders. "Fine. I'll stay put."

"Good. Now I'll be leaving you, but I'll be back to check on you in the morning. Captain wants to get an early start."

The surgeon left, taking with him Luke's hopes of seeing Melanie and the children tonight. Gingerly he laid back on the bed, shoving down his disappointment. He'd hoped to talk to her, and yes, spend a little time with the boys and the baby. His spirits sank when he thought about their arrival in Las Vegas sometime tomorrow. He dreaded having to say good-bye.

No. Not good-bye. He clenched his fists. He had something to say to Melanie all right, and it wasn't good-bye.

Leaving Melanie Faraday was the furthest thing from his mind.

"You are going to twist your handkerchief into shreds."

Melanie glanced down at the tangled cloth in her hands, and then shot Flora a scathing look. The wagon shook and swayed as it continued down the Santa Fe Trail, edging closer and closer to Las Vegas. It was the warmest day yet, and tempers were at an all time high as the six of them sweltered in the back of the wagon bed. She unwound her handkerchief and patted her face with it. "I'll shred whatever I please," she said before turning to Ramon and Raul. They had been quarreling for the past hour.

"Stop that fighting or I will spank both of you!" she snapped.

Her threat worked and they stopped immediately, shock registering on their faces. Melanie couldn't blame them. She'd even surprised herself with her outburst.

"I'm sorry boys," she said, fanning her face with the limp square of fabric. "It's the heat."

"*Si*," Ramon agreed. "It is very hot in here."

"I want to get out," Rodrigo said.

"*Tengo hambre*," Raul whined.

"We're out of food," Melanie replied. She had learned a few Spanish words during their trip, and Raul's cries of hunger were often repeated. "You'll have to wait until we're in Las Vegas."

Raul whined some more. This time she only caught the words "*Senor* Jackson."

Melanie sighed. "What did he say, Flora?"

"He wishes for *Senor* Jackson."

"So do I," Melanie muttered. But the thought of Luke had her twisting her handkerchief again and fighting back the burning sensation in her throat.

They rolled into Las Vegas later that evening.

Melanie had directed the soldiers to take them straight to the Westbrooke's. She didn't want the children to have to stay in that wagon a minute longer.

"Gather your things," she said to the boys when they had reached their final destination. "We are here at the Westbrookes."

Ramon's eyes filled with hope. "Will you be staying with us?"

"No. Flora and I have to return to Santa Fe."

His face fell. "Oh."

Her heart ached at his downcast expression.

Reluctantly he helped Rodrigo and Raul collect their few possessions. Flora placed the baby in the sling while Melanie gathered her satchel. Then they climbed out of the wagon.

The freshness of the night air was most welcome after being cooped up for so many hours. Melanie looked at the tiny adobe house in front of her, shadowed in the dusky night.

"Miss Faraday?"

The red-haired man named Rusty came up behind her. "Yes?"

"Will you be needing anything else from us, ma'am?"

Melanie's stomach twisted into a thousand tiny knots. She laid her hand across her belly as tears welled in her eyes. She thought about Luke, about the children, and how much they had all changed over the past few days.

Her mind replayed snippets of images of their journey—the flood in Pecos, Raul's scorpion sting, the Indian attack. Interspersed with those terrible moments were those she would always treasure. The look of pure joy on the boys' faces as they played in the mud. Luke's concern for Raul and the young child's tender return of devotion. Seeing Luke holding Rosalita in his strong arms, soothing her to sleep.

The kiss she'd shared with him.

How could she go back to Santa Fe without him? Without any of them? The thought of it was like daggers piercing her heart. Although she tried desperately to stop her tears, they rolled down her cheeks.

Flora moved closer to her. "*Senorita?* What is wrong?"

"I can't do this," Melanie whispered, her voice thick. "I can't leave them . . . or *him.*"

Flora nodded and laid a comforting hand on Melanie's arm. "Ah *chica,* I know it is hard. But what else can be done?"

"I can take the children back to Santa Fe with me," she said, sniffling. "Father will just have to accept them."

"After you have brought them all the way out here? And what if your Father says no? It would be unfair for the little ones to make this journey twice."

"I know . . . I know." Dejected, Melanie wiped

her eyes with her handkerchief and looked at the boys. They were silent and solemn. "I love them so much," she said softly.

"And *Senor* Jackson?"

She paused. "Yes, Flora. I love him too." The realization brought a shaky smile to her face, only to fade with her next words. "But it's all for naught, isn't it?"

"Maybe. Maybe not."

Melanie's eyes widened. "What do you mean?"

Flora held up her hands. "If there is one thing I know about you, *chica*, it is that you go after what you want. You will do anything for those you love."

Melanie pondered her words. What could she possibly do to change their situation? It was completely out of her hands now.

And then it came to her. At first the idea seemed completely preposterous. But the more she thought about it, the more valid it became. *At least it's worth a try.*

"Miss Faraday? Is there anything else you need?" Rusty repeated.

Turning toward him, she smiled, brushing the tears from her cheek with the back of her hand. "Yes," she said, a tiny thread of hope weaving through her. "There is something you can do. Take us into town."

"Pardon me?"

"We want to go into town," she stated, more firmly this time. She wrapped her arms around the three boys and drew them close, then motioned for Flora and Rosalita. "All of us."

"What?" Flora exclaimed when Melanie told her about her plan an hour later, after they'd settled in the small villa she had rented in the center of Las Vegas.

"It's the only way for all of us to be together," Melanie said, holding her hands palms up.

Flora's brows knitted together. "But marriage? You want to ask *Senor* Jackson to marry you?"

"Yes. For the sake of the children, of course," she added.

"Of course," Flora remarked dryly as if she didn't believe Melanie's statement at all.

"I know Luke cares for them very much, and his family owns a sheep farm in Texas. It would be a wonderful place to raise children."

"True," Flora said. However, doubt colored her tone. "But it is a lot to ask of him, don't you think? To marry and adopt four children?"

Four Mexican children. Melanie didn't voice her thoughts out loud, but she had to take that into consideration. Just because he cared for the boys and Rosalita, didn't mean he would welcome them into his family.

"And have you forgotten you are to marry *Senor* Vincent? What will you do about that?"

"I'll have to explain it to Father . . . somehow."

"And to *Senor* Jackson as well." Flora shook her head. "Are you sure you want to do this? Maybe you should think about it for a little while."

"What is there to think about? I don't really have any other choice."

Flora studied her for a moment, and gave Melanie a small smile. She placed her hand on Melanie's arm. "Then I wish you good luck," she said, before walking to the tiny kitchen area.

Melanie sat down on the hard wooden chair near the scuffed dining table, gathering courage for what she had to do. The night before she had asked Rusty where the Army was making camp. She was pleased to find out they were only on the outskirts of town. Luke wasn't that far away. But the regiment would stay only a day longer, to rest up and buy supplies. Then they would head on to Fort Bent. In the morning she would find Luke, explain her situation with Ethan Vincent and how she was breaking the engagement, then offer Luke her proposal.

A little spark of excitement lit within her as she remembered what Luke had said about their kiss. *I didn't mind it at all.* She smiled. Perhaps, over time, he could learn to love her just a little bit.

But even if that never came to pass, she could live with it. She would be with Luke and the children, and that would be enough.

She had more than enough love for all of them.

Chapter Seventeen

Standing outside his tent, Luke took a few practice steps with his crutches, trying to get the feel of
walking on them again. It didn't take long, as he'd
used a pair before when he was shot in the leg. Soon
he was moving around on them easily. He searched
around the Army campsite, looking for Rusty.

It wasn't long before he found him. "Where is
Miss Faraday?" Luke asked.

"Well, it was the strangest thing, sir." Rusty lifted
his hat and wiped his damp forehead with the cuff
of his sleeve. "Earl and me went to drop her off at
that Westbrooke house, but no sooner had they got
out of the wagon did they climb back in, wanting to
leave."

"What?" Luke asked in amazement.

"Just like I said. Miss Faraday and the rest of them are staying at a house in town."

What was she up to? He grinned. Whatever it was, he would bet his good leg it had been a spur of the moment decision. "Can you take me over there?" he asked Rusty.

"Over to Miss Faraday's? Tonight?"

"Yes. Right now." He had to find out what was going on. And while he was doing that, he could talk to her about the future . . . their future together. "I need your help, Rusty. I can't seat a horse with this leg."

"I'll have to check with the captain."

"I'll wait right here."

Rusty took off to find Captain Davis. While the soldier was gone, Luke sank deep into his own thoughts.

He'd had lots of time to himself during their journey from Tecolote to Las Vegas. Time to think, and time to miss Melanie. He missed the children too. He'd felt so empty the last couple of days without their company.

It simply supported what he'd realized back in Tecolote—he couldn't leave the New Mexico Territory without them. She was headstrong, impulsive, and brave beyond measure. And he loved her, there was no denying it. He wanted to bring Melanie home with him to San Antonio—as his wife. If she was willing, he wanted to bring the children home too.

He gripped the crutches. Now all he had to do was get to her, propose, and hope she'd say yes. He knew deep in his heart there was something between them. Maybe it wasn't love on her part, but she could learn to love him. Even if she didn't, he would still love her.

It was all so remarkable. Never would he have imagined falling in love with Melanie Faraday. Neither could he have conceived of the idea of adopting four Mexican children. Yet when he thought about his life without them, he couldn't stand it.

A few minutes later Rusty returned. "The captain has no problem with it. There's a livery nearby, I'll get a cart."

"Thanks. I owe you one." Anticipation raced through him. He couldn't wait to see Melanie. To talk to her. To take her in his arms and kiss her, showing her feelings he couldn't express in words. Then he would ask her to marry him.

He prayed she would say yes.

Melanie poured cool water from a pitcher into the porcelain basin on the washstand. The children were already in bed, and Flora had also retired for the night. Dipping a cloth into the water, she rung it out and scrubbed the trail dust from her neck and face. She undid her hair, brushed and plaited it into a long braid down her back. "There," she said out loud, even though she was the only one in the room. "Much better."

But she didn't feel any better.

Placing a hand on her fluttering stomach, she tried to steady her nerves. It was impossible. Her insides flipped and flopped like a fish struggling to live on dry land. But she supposed her reaction was to be expected.

She'd never proposed to a man before.

How would she get any sleep tonight, knowing what lay ahead for her in the morning? She was both thrilled and terrified. Reaching for her nightgown, she started to put it on, but changed her mind. The last thing she wanted to do was lay in bed stewing in her own thoughts.

She tiptoed into the sitting room, the quiet of the house overwhelming. She wasn't used to it. There had been constant noise on the trail. The sounds of children playing, talking, arguing. Rosalita's cooing and crying. The crunch of the wagon wheels over dry clods of dirt. The soothing music of nocturnal animals in the evenings. Now there was just . . . silence.

"Senorita?"

She turned at the sound of Flora's voice. "I'm sorry," she said. "Did I wake you?"

Flora shook her head. "No. I cannot sleep. It is too quiet."

Melanie smiled. "I was thinking that exact same thing."

"I will make us a snack."

"Gracias." Melanie walked over to a chair and sat down. She toyed with the buttons on her shirtwaist. "I don't know if I can do this," she whispered.

Flora glanced up from the tortilla she was rolling into a small tube. "Do what, *chica?*"

"Explain everything to my father. Take care of four children." She sighed and looked at Flora. "Ask Luke to marry me."

A smile formed on Flora's face. "You can, *senorita*. You are a strong woman . . . you have proved that on this journey. But I must ask this—do you still believe asking *Senor* Jackson to marry you is the right thing to do?"

Melanie nodded without hesitation.

"Then do it. Trust yourself, and trust *Senor* Jackson. Believe in the love you have for him."

Rising from her chair, Melanie circled her arms around Flora and hugged her. *"Gracias,"* she murmured against her cheek. "For everything."

A hard knock sounded at the door. The women pulled apart.

"I wonder who that could be?" Melanie said, bewildered that someone would call on them at this late hour.

Flora answered the door. Melanie's heart leapt as soon as she heard his deep, rich voice.

"Is Miss Faraday in?"

Luke!

Chapter Eighteen

Although more than anything Melanie wanted to run to him, her feet refused to cooperate. Flora moved to the side. Melanie's palms grew damp when she saw him.

"Hi," he said softly.

His appearance had changed dramatically. He'd bathed and shaved, and somehow managed to clean the numerous layers of dust off his hat. His dark eyes sparkled with warmth, seeming to penetrate her very core. His presence made her giddy inside.

"Hi," she finally replied, still awestruck at how handsome he was.

"Um, Melanie?"

"Yes?"

"May I come in? I'm not real steady on these things."

For the first time she realized he was on crutches. Her face heated up. "Yes, yes, of course. I'm sorry, come in. How is your leg?" she asked as he hobbled his way inside.

"Improving." He stopped a few inches from her and met her gaze. "It'll take more than a little arrow to keep me down."

She smiled, his good mood calming her a bit. Gesturing to one of the crude chairs, she said, "Sit down, please."

He sank into the chair, his large frame filling it.

"I'm sorry we don't have better furniture," she said, casting a quick glance at the room's sparse furnishings.

"I'm fine. I have to admit, after sitting on a buck-seat for so long, this feels good." He removed his hat.

Melanie sat down in the chair across from him, suddenly at a loss for what to say. He was right here in front of her, the moment was hers for the taking. She'd practiced her proposal over and over the past few hours in anticipation for tomorrow. But he was here now. Why couldn't she get the words out of her mouth?

"I heard you didn't leave the children," he said.

She nodded, grateful for the shift in subject. "You heard correctly."

"But why? I thought that was the whole purpose for this trip, to find them a new home."

"I know, I know." She paused, glancing down at her lap. "I just couldn't do it. I couldn't leave them behind." She looked at him. "You probably think I'm a silly twit that wasted your time."

He shook his head. "No. Just the opposite. I know you care about them a lot. I do too." Luke leaned forward a bit, fixing his eyes on her. "I think it's time we talked," he said in a voice that would melt a block of butter.

It left her mouth as dry as cotton. "I—it is?"

He nodded, still staring at her. "About the children . . . and about us." He caressed her face with his tender gaze. His eyes were filled with an emotion she couldn't define, one that made her feel cherished. Wanted. *Loved.*

He looked at his bad leg and frowned. "Curse this injury," he said, looking back at her. "I wanted to do this all proper-like, but it can't be helped." He reached for her hand. "Melanie, I know this is going to sound crazy. We haven't known each other that long, but I think there's something between us. Um, a connection, or something like that." He swallowed.

At that moment she knew what he wanted to talk about. Joy flowed through her, but it was tempered by the one secret still between them. She had to tell him about Ethan. Before she could speak with him about anything, she had to be completely honest. "Luke, before you say anything else, there's something I have to tell you—"

He raised his hand. "If I don't say this now I may never get the words out." He took a deep breath. "Melanie Faraday, I love you. And believe it or not, I love those children too. I want us to be a family." He gripped her hand with both of his own. "Will you marry me?"

Melanie's eyes widened. He loved her? He loved the children? Had she actually heard him right?

"Say something, darlin'," he prodded, squeezing her hand. "Don't leave me hanging out on a limb here."

Hope shined brightly in his eyes, tearing at her heart. Why oh why hadn't she told him about Ethan before now? How would he react to finding out she was engaged to someone else?

"Melanie?" he said, the hope fading quickly away. "Is there something wrong?"

"Not exactly," she started.

He sat back in the chair. "You don't love me."

"No, no! I do love you, Luke." She leaned forward and touched his face. "I love you with all my heart."

His expression lightened a little. "Then what's the problem? I know moving to San Antonio is a lot to ask—"

"That's not it either. I know I'll love San Antonio.

I'll love anywhere you and the children are." She licked her lips. "Luke, I know I should have told you this before, but it never seemed to be the right time. I mean, I never expected this to happen, to fall in love with you and everything. Keeping the children was hardly a possibility either, so the subject never came up while we were on the trail. On the other hand, I suppose I could have said something—"

"Melanie, stop," he said forcefully. "You're rambling."

"I know." She wrung her hands. "I can't help it."

"Just tell me," he said softly. "Whatever it is, I'll understand."

"Oh Lord, I hope so," she mumbled. "Luke, I want to marry you, more than anything I've ever wanted in my life. But before we can get married, I have to do something first."

"What's that?"

"Break off my engagement with my fiancé."

"Your *what*?" Luke thought his head was about to explode. Either that or his heart.

"My fiancé." Melanie shot up from the chair and began to pace. "See, the situation isn't what it appears to be—"

"You're engaged?" He sat back in his chair, dumbfounded. "Engaged? To be married?"

"Yes, but not really."

He looked at her through narrowed eyes, anger welling inside him. "How can you 'not really' be engaged? You either are or you aren't."

"I am, but not for long." She stopped pacing and knelt down beside him. "As soon as we return to Santa Fe I'm going to break off my engagement with Ethan."

"Unbelievable." He thrust his hand through his hair. "How could you not tell me this before?"

"Like I said, the time never seemed right."

"And this time does? I bare my heart and soul to you, ask you to be my wife, and you choose this moment to tell me you belong to another man?"

"I don't *belong* to anyone," she insisted, her nostrils flaring.

He couldn't believe she had the nerve to act insulted. She was the one who deceived him. "You said you loved me."

"I do."

"How can you when you're set to marry someone else?"

"I told you, I'm breaking the engagement."

"Oh no, not on my account you aren't." He grabbed his crutches. "I won't be blamed for busting up your relationship."

"Luke, Ethan and I don't have a relationship. That's what I'm trying to tell you."

But he was done listening. Done being stupid.

She'd lied to him from the very beginning—about the boys, about her reason for the trip. And now about this. He wouldn't be made a fool of anymore.

Suddenly the front door burst open with a re-sounding bang. Melanie jumped.

Flora hurried into the room. "*Senor* Faraday!" she said with a gasp.

Melanie's gaze shot to the doorway. "Father?"

Chapter Nineteen

"Melanie!" Herman Faraday rushed into the room and engulfed his daughter in a big hug. "I've been worried sick about you." He stepped back, running his hands down her arms and searching her face. "Are you alright? What in the blazes made you do something so foolish?" Before she could answer he embraced her again. "It doesn't matter, I'm just glad to see you."

Luke took in the emotions between father and daughter. He was a short man, just a few inches taller than Melanie. Their affection for each other was readily apparent. If he was angry with her, he didn't show it. He seemed more relieved than upset.

"Father, what are you doing here?" Melanie asked as Herman released her.

"Coming to find you." He glanced past Melanie's shoulder, noticing Luke for the first time. His eyes squinted slightly as he scrutinized Luke. "Perhaps you should introduce me to your guest."

"Oh, y-yes," she stammered, appearing completely flustered. Two spots of rosy-red colored her cheeks. "Father, this is Mr. Luke Jackson, a soldier in the American Army. He escorted us here to Las Vegas."

"Mr. Jackson," Herman said with a curt nod. After a pause he extended his hand, and his expression softened a bit. "Thank you. I appreciate you keeping my daughter safe on this wild excursion of hers."

Luke nodded, his lips pressed tightly.

"You're injured," Herman said, looking at Luke's leg. "What happened?"

Luke gave him a condensed, clipped version of the events, his story sparking alarm in Herman Faraday's light blue eyes. He turned to Melanie. "You were attacked by Indians?"

"Only two."

"*Only* two? You could have been hurt, or killed." He removed his expensive looking hat, exposing his half-bald pate. Brown and gray hair lay damp around the top of his ears. "I was so afraid for you, dear. As soon as I read your note, we immediately left Santa Fe."

"We?" Melanie asked, a strange look on her face.

"Yes. Ethan is with me. He's putting up the

horses and coach right now. I'm afraid we ran the poor beasts ragged, but we had to find you."

Luke gripped his crutches as the color drained completely from Melanie's face. "Ethan is here?" she repeated feebly.

"Why, yes, he was worried about you. We both were."

At that moment a distinguished looking man with a thick, dark mustache walked through the door. His clothes were dusty and disheveled, but Luke could tell they were expensive. He appeared to be a little older than Melanie. His gray eyes lit up as soon as he saw her.

"Miss Faraday!" he said, hurrying to her. He doffed his hat. "Thank God you are safe. We were worried about you."

"I heard," she mumbled.

While Melanie seemed in shock, Luke was angry. Angry and bitter, and more than ready to get out of there. He started to stand, using his crutches for support.

"Oh, Mr. Jackson," Herman said, coming over to him. "You must think me terribly rude. Let me introduce you to Ethan Vincent. Melanie's fiancé."

Those mere words made Luke feel like he'd been hit in the gut with a hundred Indian arrows. He could barely muster a nod of notice toward the other man. "I'll be going now," he said, barely able to contain his fury. He clutched the handles of his crutches and headed for the door.

"Luke, wait," she called out.

"Luke?" he heard Ethan say. "You're using his Christian name, Miss Faraday?"

"Just what happened on this trip?" Herman asked, sounding suspicious.

Luke didn't bother to explain. He had to get out of there before he said something he'd regret. Before his heart broke into a million fragments in front of Melanie and her precious fiancé. He walked out the door. Without looking back.

"Luke, please, let me explain."

Melanie followed him outside. He was moving remarkably quickly on his crutches, obviously more than eager to get away from her. She couldn't blame him. She wouldn't blame him if he never wanted to speak to her again. Still, she had to try to talk to him. "Please, Luke, *stop*."

To her surprise he did. He turned around, and his expression almost did her in. Anger, hurt, betrayal, it was all there, screaming at her from behind his eyes. She wanted to cry, and not because he was mad at her.

She wanted to weep because of what she'd done to him.

She went to him, ignoring the fact that Ethan and

her father were standing in the doorway of the villa, watching everything unfold. She didn't care what they saw or how they reacted to it. All she cared about was making Luke understand . . . if it was even possible. "I'm sorry," she started.

"Sure. Right. You're always sorry, aren't you?"

"I deserve that. And more."

He shook his head. "I am such a fool. Pledging my undying love to a woman who . . . who . . ."

"Doesn't deserve it." Tears started to flow and she wiped them from her cheeks.

"You said it, not me." He pinned her with a pointed glare. "Tell the children I said good-bye."

She lifted her chin. "You tell them yourself. Don't break their hearts because of this."

"Like you broke mine?" He nodded in Ethan's direction. "Have a happy life, Miss Faraday. It's time I got on with my own." With that he turned and limped away.

Anguish welled up inside her. She wanted to run after him, to beg his forgiveness, to plead with him to take her back. But she didn't. There was no reason to. She'd hurt him by not being completely honest with him. She didn't blame him for leaving.

He had every right to.

"Here. Drink this."

Melanie took the steaming cup of tea from

Ethan's outstretched hand. They were sitting on the long bench underneath the awning in front of the villa. "You shouldn't be this nice to me," she mumbled bitterly. "I just broke off our engagement."

"What else could you do?"

"I've really messed things up." Melanie watched the breeze kick up swirls of clay dust on the dirt road leading to the house. "I lied to my father, to you, to the Army, to Luke . . ." She sighed. "Not that I would expect you to understand."

"I understand more than you think, Miss Faraday. Actually, you did me a favor."

She turned to him. "I did?"

"Yes. Our fathers set up this betrothal as a business arrangement. But that's not what I want from a marriage. I don't think you do either."

She shook her head. "No."

"You're not the only one who loves someone else." Melancholy tinged his tone. He stood up. "I'll be staying at the hotel in town, and leaving for San Francisco in the morning."

Rising, she turned and looked at him. A wistful expression filled his face. "Did she hurt you?" Melanie asked, knowing she was being terribly nosy, but needing to ask him just the same.

"No," he said, shaking his head. "Nothing like that." He stared off into the distance. "I hope things work out between you and Mr. Jackson. I have a feeling they will." He placed his hat on his head, tipped it toward her, then walked away.

As Ethan mounted his horse, Melanie thought about what he'd said. *I hope you're right, Mr. Vincent. In fact, I pray that you are.*

Chapter Twenty

"Melanie, darling. I hate to see you so despondent."

Melanie stared out of the window of her father's coach as it rolled down the Santa Fe Trail. Behind them was a second coach, with Ramon, Rosalita and Flora inside. She glanced at Raul, who was falling asleep next to her. Rodrigo had already slipped into slumber several minutes ago as he sat beside her father.

Herman Faraday hadn't blinked an eye when Melanie explained the situation concerning the children over breakfast that morning. "If only you had come to me before all this Melanie," he'd said. "I would have understood. You didn't have to run away."

"I wasn't running away," she insisted.

"Weren't you?" He placed his fork down on the table, letting his eggs turn cold. "I'm afraid it's my fault. If I hadn't promised you to Vincent—"

"Father, I made these mistakes, not you. I take responsibility for them. And I promise I will take responsibility for the children."

"I know you will. You'll be a wonderful mother to them."

Recalling the conversation brought a tiny smile to her lips, but it quickly disappeared as fear of the unknown took its place. Her father's confidence and kindness aside, she was still the primary caregiver of these four children. She loved them so much. She just hoped she wouldn't fail them. *Like I failed Luke.*

She looked out the window and tried to push him from her mind. He would be heading for San Antonio soon, if he wasn't already on his way. Sadness overcame her. Would she spend the rest of her life thinking about him? Wondering if he married and had children? Hoping he was happy?

She knew she always would.

The coach ran over a large bump, bringing Melanie out of her thoughts. Thinking about Luke's future happiness did nothing to repair the vacant feeling inside her. She missed him terribly.

"Please, tell me what is troubling you," her father

prodded. "Is it Ethan? Maybe you were too hasty in annulling your betrothal."

"No, Father. He and I both agreed it was for the best."

"Then what is it?"

She turned from him and looked out the window again. "It's nothing, Father. Nothing at all."

They camped in Tecolote that night. Not only had her father hired extra guards for the trip, but also a cook and a young man to assist with setting up camp. Melanie had to admit it was nice not to have to worry about the meal, to just concentrate solely on the children for once. She changed Rosalita, played with Raul, and teased Rodrigo and Ramon. Anything to keep the memories of the last time they were here at bay.

A short while later the sun was setting in the west, casting a pinkish glow over the mountains and grassy field. Melanie sat in front of the fire, staring at the orange flames. Everyone else had turned in early. She felt a hand on her shoulder, and placed her own on top of it.

"*Chica,* you must find happiness on your own," Flora said. "For the children's sake."

"What if I can't?" Melanie's voice cracked as she removed her hand from Flora's. "I try not to think about him. But I can't help it."

"I know, I know. It will take time. But focusing on the children will help, I think." Flora moved to face her. "Come to bed, Melanie. You look very tired."

"I will in a little bit. I just want some time alone."

"All right. *Buenos noches.*"

"*Buenos noches,* Flora."

She didn't know how long she sat there, letting the fire lull her into peace. Finally she rose, ready to head for bed, when she heard the faint sound of hoof beats in the distance.

Fear gripped her as her mind flashed back to the day the rogue Indians had attacked them. Without hesitation she crept to the coach and found the small pistol her father kept hidden in a wooden box under the driver's seat. As the pounding of the galloping horse filled her ears, she checked the gun for bullets and whirled around, ready to shoot.

"Stop right where you are!" she shouted as the horse entered their camp.

The rider slowed down, the dim light obscuring her view of him. She aimed the gun directly at his chest. "I know how to use this."

"I know you do." The rider held up his hands in surrender.

"Luke?" she said, shock pulsing through her. She squinted. "Is it really you?"

"Put that thing down and I'll prove it."

She lowered the gun, and he gingerly dismounted

the horse. She could see his crutches tied to the back of the animal, but he didn't reach for them. Instead he limped toward her.

He tipped his hat as calmly as if they'd never fought, as if they'd never been separated more than a minute. "Miss Faraday."

"Mr. Jackson," she said hoarsely.

Removing his hat, he looked down at her. Their eyes locked, and everything that had come between them in the past instantly melted away.

With a cry she ran into his arms and pressed her face against his chest. "I missed you," she sobbed, ashamed by her tears but helpless to stop them. "I can't believe you're here."

"Miss Faraday! Is everything alright?"

She turned around and saw her father's men rushing toward her, armed.

"Wait, wait," she called out, holding up her hands. "I know this man. We're not in danger."

"Well praise the Lord for that," the cook said, lowering his rifle. One red suspender loop hung from his waist, the other one halfway pulled up his arm. "We heard the horse and thought it was an ambush."

"Mr. Jackson?" Herman came toward them, the hair on the sides of his head sticking out in all directions. "What are you doing here?"

"I was hoping to have a word with your daughter," Luke replied, looking at Melanie. "If she'll let me, that is."

"I don't know," Herman started.

"Father, its okay." She gazed up at Luke.

Herman cleared his throat. "Well, ah, I guess that's settled then. Men, secure the camp." He glanced back at Melanie for a moment, then walked toward his bedroll.

When they were alone, Luke led her toward the fire, his gait uneven because of his injured leg. He didn't say anything. He simply embraced her again, the rapid thumping of his heart in her ear telling her everything she needed to know.

He'd missed her too.

"I couldn't leave you," he said, leaning his chin on the top of her head. "I tried. I headed for Fort Bent, ready to get my discharge papers so I could go home to San Antonio. I did everything I could to put you out of my mind." He drew her from him and looked into her eyes. "But in your usual stubborn way, you wouldn't disappear. So I figured I had only one choice. To come after you."

"Oh, Luke," she said. "I'm so—"

He pressed his finger against her lips. "You don't have to say it. I already know. I'm sorry too."

"You have nothing to be sorry for. I hurt you. I'm in the wrong. I should have told you about my engagement from the beginning."

Releasing her, he stepped away. "There's just one thing I have to know before we go any further." He sucked in a deep breath. "Are you still marrying him?"

"Ethan?"

"Yeah. Ethan."

She smiled. "No. We called it off after you left. But I was planning to break it off with him long before that. I don't love him, I never did. We were only betrothed because my father arranged it."

"Your father wasn't upset about it, was he?"

"No. He only wants me to be happy."

For the first time since he arrived, Luke grinned. "And just what is it that makes you happy, *senorita?*"

"You, Luke Jackson." She moved closer to him. "You make me happy."

He leaned forward and pressed his mouth to hers. The kiss whisked her breath away.

They drew apart and he touched his forehead to hers. "I was hoping to hear that. Melanie, I'm not a man for a lot of flowery words and all that junk. So I'm just going to say this flat out. I love you. I simply . . . love you."

Her heart hammered against her ribcage. She almost couldn't believe she was hearing the words again. Yet the emotion was there, not only in what he said but in the way he gazed at her, the way his eyes told her beautiful things words couldn't express.

"Oh my," she finally breathed. Her mouth spread into a wide smile. "I love you too, Luke Jackson. With all my heart and soul, I love you."

They both laughed. When their mirth faded, he reached for her hand and held it. "I want to kiss you again. But I think I'll wait."

Disappointed, her mouth pursed. "Why?"

He winked at her. "There will be plenty of time for that later," he said. "Especially after we're married."

"Married?" She felt faint. "You still want to marry me?"

"That's what people in love do, Melanie." He paused, cupping her chin with his hand. "Will you marry me?"

"Yes," she said without hesitation. "I'll marry you."

He lifted her up in his arms, as if he couldn't feel his injury at all. "Forget it," he said, bringing his mouth closer to hers. "I can't wait that long to kiss you again."

After breaking the kiss, he set her down. "Are you sure about this?" he asked.

"Absolutely."

"You'll have to move to San Antonio."

"I know. I'll move anywhere you want me to, Luke. Texas, New Mexico, even California if you want."

"Hold on a minute," he said, laughing. "Texas will be just fine." Then he grew serious. "But what about the children? Are they still with you?"

"Yes. They're still with me."

"I want to adopt them, darlin'. I want us to be a family. That is, if you're alright with that."

She nodded fiercely and cradled his face in both of her hands, then kissed him hard. "I love you," she whispered against his mouth. "I love you so much."

He leaned forward and kissed her back. "I can't seem to stop doing that, Mrs. Jackson."

She laughed gaily. "Mrs. Jackson . . . I like the sound of that."

He drew her against him, tightening his arms around her. "So do I, sweetheart," he murmured in her ear. "So do I."

... 1 2 ...
= = 2010

2009

2005